If you wish escape, show

I looked at Donnelly. He had moved back from the spy-window; he was lighting a cigarette, frowning at the match-flame. His mouth was sullen.

I put my left hand flat against the window. I thought, *I'm dreaming*.

The interviewer said querulously, ". . . getting us no-where. Can't you—"

"Wait," said the buzzing voice. "Let me say, please. Ignorant man hold (*blink*) burning stick, say, this is breath (*blink*) of the wood. Then you show him flashlight—"

I took a deep breath, and held it.

Around the alien, four men went down together, folding over quietly at waist and knee, sprawling on the floor. I heard a thump behind me.

Donnelly was lying stretched out along the wall, his head tilted against the corner. The cigarette had fallen from his hand.

I looked back at Aza-Kra. His head turned slightly, the dark flesh crinkling. Two eyes stared back at me through the window.

"Now you can breathe," said the monster.

—from *Rule Golden*

Other Tor books by Damon Knight

DAMON KNIGHT

RULE GOLDEN

&

DOUBLE MEANING

TOR

A TOM DOHERTY ASSOCIATES BOOK
NEW YORK

Tor SF Double No. 34

RULE GOLDEN

DOUBLE MEANING

A Tor Book
Published by Tom Doherty Associates, Inc.
49 West 24th Street
New York, N.Y. 10010

Cover art by Wayne Barlow

ISBN: 0-812-51294-4

First edition: May 1991

Printed in the United States of America

0 9 8 7 6 5 4 3 2 1

INTRODUCTION

Beauty, Stupidity, Injustice, and Science Fiction

I ENCOUNTERED BEAUTY IN THE PERSON OF MY FIRST-GRADE teacher, Miss Cellars. She was in her twenties, slender, dark-haired, graceful and fragrant. I was six years old; I was as thunderstruck as any mooncalf adolescent.

After a few days some of us were transferred to a class taught by the principal, Mrs. Cornelius, familiarly known as Old Lady Corncob. There I encountered stupidity and injustice.

Roaming the aisles one day, Mrs. Cornelius found me coloring a milk bottle white. "Now you *know* milk isn't white, it's *yellow*," she told me.

I encountered science fiction in the August–September 1933 issue of *Amazing Stories*. I was eleven years old. I had read all the fairy tales in the public library, and all the Oz books I could find, and *Alice*, and the Pooh books, and *Wind in the Willows*, and I loved them; but I saw at once that *Amazing Stories* was better because the stories were scientific and therefore might someday be true, and also because their repertory was immensely larger than that of fantasy.

In these stories, men shrank themselves so small that they could explore the surface of an electron, or made monsters from synthetic protoplasm in jello molds, or found out how to transmit flavors by radio. They built giant robots that went crashing through Manhattan, and spherical spaceships that zoomed off at the speed of light; they traveled backward, forward, and sidewise in time. There was no end to it, no fear (yet) that you would find any story like any other story.

On our family's occasional trips to Portland, I spent my hoarded allowance (fifteen cents a week, but a penny was worth something then) on wonderful old bedsheet-sized *Amazing*s and *Wonder*s. Working my way back from the issues I already had, I discovered that magazine science fiction had been invented in 1926 by a man named Hugo Gernsback.

Gernsback liked to explain in his editorials that "scientifiction" would transform the world by teaching young people to appreciate the wonders of science. And, in fact, it was from science fiction that I got my life-long fascination with science. I never could have been infected with it by the mind-numbing science courses in junior high and high school, during which I spent as much time as I could reading Thorne Smith behind a textbook.

Early on, to exhibit what he meant by "scientifiction" and to fill the pages cheaply, Gernsback reprinted many works by H. G. Wells and other foreign authors. I learned that Wells was the father of what was now called science fiction. I began ordering his books through the local library, and read them all, even *The Sea Lady* and *The Shape of Things to Come*.

In 1934, during a trip to Portland in which we were quarantined in a hotel because I had the measles, I read my first issue of *Astounding Stories*, a magazine I had never seen before. It was a different size, the covers were brighter and the stories were more exciting.

Astounding was started in 1931 by William Clayton, who published a string of pulp magazines under his own banner. His innovation, as important as anything Campbell did later, was to treat science fiction as just another kind of pulp, emphasizing action, mystery and adventure.

Clayton sold his magazines to Street & Smith in 1933. Under its new editors, F. Orlin Tremaine and Desmond Hall, *Astounding* aggressively recruited the most popular s.f. writers, undersold and outpromoted the competition, and effectively drove it from the field. Gernsback's failing *Wonder Stories* was sold to the Standard chain in 1936 and became *Thrilling Wonder*, a dismal publication just above the level of comic books. *Amazing Stories*, which Gernsback had sold to Teck Publications in 1929, was sold again in 1938 and became the stamping ground of Chicago writers nobody had ever heard of before. The new editor, Raymond A. Palmer, published a series of rambling narratives by Richard S. Shaver, who claimed to have discovered a race of malevolent creatures living in caves deep underground and zapping the surface-dwellers with mind rays.

In high school, the Latin teacher gave us a series of statements in Latin to be marked true or false. One was "Pueri sunt parves homines." I marked it T. When I got the paper back, the teacher had checked that off as wrong. I asked her why; she said with a smile, "Boys aren't little men, they're *boys*."

Even in the first grade, I could not help noticing that some of the other students were dolts, and when I got to junior high I discovered that some of the teachers were no better. I learned very early that if I took the opposite opinion from that of my elders and teachers, I could be sure of being right at least ninety-nine percent of the time. I have held this as a principle ever since, and it has served me very well. In science fiction, ironically enough, my model was what John Campbell called his "Yes? Well, let's see now . . ." stories. ("It would be awful to be conquered by invaders from another planet. Yes? Well, let's see now . . .")

John W. Campbell, Jr., became the editor of *Astounding* in 1938 and immediately set about transforming it from the roots. Campbell was the first s.f. magazine editor who was a professional s.f. writer (with the dubious exception of Hugo Gernsback, who had published a creaky novel called *Ralph 124C41+);* he was the second s.f. magazine editor who was trained in science (the first was T. O'Conor Sloane, an antediluvian chemist who did not believe space travel would ever become a reality). Campbell began putting together a stable of writers who could write about real science and real scientists (not the mad ones in drafty castles we had had before). Among these were Isaac Asimov, L. Sprague de Camp, and Robert A. Heinlein, the fathers of modern science fiction. This phase did not last very long. Campbell wanted an adult s.f. magazine, but he found out that many of his readers didn't.

In 1939 I expected the Campbell revolution to continue forever; I did not understand the forces that drive exceptional efforts back toward mediocrity. One of these forces is the need to sell magazines. The first duty of an editor is to keep his magazine alive, even if that means compromising its vision.

Another is the need for change and variety to hold the readers' attention. If you have something good and change it, it may not be for the better; but a magazine that doesn't evolve will probably die.

Then there is enthusiasm: when something new is being created, it is very high, but that doesn't last. And finally there is the second law of thermodynamics, otherwise known as entropy. When I was editing *Orbit* and was lucky enough to find four or five superb writers almost at once, I thought their presence would attract others equally brilliant and productive, and so on ad infinitum, but it didn't happen. There is no law that says aces have to keep turning up, or that good writers have to be born at a steady rate: indeed, they seem to come in clusters. This fact enables critics to divide literature into "periods," and write learnedly about the differences between them.

In 1940, when I was a student at the WPA Art Center in Salem, another student took me to see a piece of sculpture that had been recently put up in Roosevelt Park in Portland, overlooking the waterfront. It was a sandstone monolith, about thirty feet tall on its pedestal: a stylized human figure with its hands on the hilt of a sword standing upright against the body, point on the ground. It doesn't sound like much now, but seen against water and sky it gave me my first intense esthetic experience not connected with the presence of a woman's body.

The Portland women's club hated it, and a year or so later, when some work was being done in the park, a bull-dozer accidentally knocked it down.

My literary idols are Robert Graves, Aldous Huxley, Mark Twain, Ernest Hemingway, John O'Hara, Dashiell Hammett, George Orwell, Arthur Koestler, John Collier, and Rudyard Kipling. In science fiction, I have learned from John Campbell (in his Don A. Stuart mode), from L. Sprague de Camp, from Robert A. Heinlein, from Murray Leinster, from Eric Frank Russell, and from Henry Kuttner and C. L. Moore.

Precision, sense of form, playfulness, restraint and irony are the qualities I admire in all these writers. In science fiction, they are Golden Age Campbell writers, every one.

Under his own name Campbell wrote heavy-handed Smithian space-war epics, full of violent overnight inventions and crashing sparks. As Don A. Stuart, he gave himself the freedom to write something different. "Twilight," "Night," "Forgetfulness," and "Dead Knowledge" are mood stories, as Campbell said they were, and the mood is one of wistful regret—at the opposite pole from the cheerful hell-with-you optimism of the fiction Campbell wrote under his own name and later promoted in *Astounding*.

Even before the Golden Age, Campbell was working toward the rapprochement of science fiction and literature which we are still uneasily attempting fifty years later. So were the writers he gathered around him from 1938 to 1941. If he had not abandoned this effort later in the forties, how far along would we be now?

I wanted to get out of Oregon, preferably to a world city where I thought I might find somebody to talk to. I would have preferred Paris because of its French girls, but New York would do, and when the Futurians invited me to join them, I went. The moment I got there, I felt like a dragonfly just out of its chrysalis.

Much later, when I went back to Hood River on a visit, I found that an astonishing number of my classmates had married each other and stayed put for thirty years. I drove by my old house; the white wood siding had been covered with asbestos shingles, and all the cherry trees had been cut down.

In 1942 the Japanese-American residents of Oregon and other western states were rounded up and sent to prison camps. Among them were the parents of Roku Yasui, my childhood friend. He was away at school in the east. His sister Michi, a student at the University of Oregon, stood at the railroad station in Eugene and watched the train with her parents on it rolling by.

I was in New York then, but I read the local newspaper and discovered that merchants in Hood River had put up signs: NO JAPS. The names of Nisei servicemen had been erased from the plaque in the middle of the town where they had lived all their lives.

In my boyhood I had read the supermasculine epics of E. E. Smith and Charles Willard Diffin with pleasure (and I also read the Tarzan books, and the historical romances of Raphael Sabatini).

As I grew older I began to realize that the heroic models in these stories were not merely unrealistic but pernicious, and that the same was true of the evil villains, who in my boyhood were usually Orientals.

By dividing the characters into good and evil, these stories fostered an us-against-them mentality, and taught us that the good people had English, Scotch, or Irish names and were tall, blond and blue-eyed, and that the bad people had dark skins and hair in order to make them readily identifiable, just as the bad people in Western movies wore black hats.

Such blatant racism is seldom seen nowadays, but the

underlying attitudes have not changed. In much adventure science fiction, the heroes are still tall blond supermen, and the villains are Asians disguised as aliens by the change of two letters.

Wells himself has much to answer for. His *War of the Worlds* began the tradition of slimy invading monsters from other worlds. *Things to Come*, for which he wrote the screenplay, glorifies the protoNazi airmen of ''Wings Over the World,'' and closes with a hymn to the brave Anglo spacefarers who will conquer the universe for Man.

Significantly, the only character in the film who does not have a British name and face is the villain of the final episode, the sculptor who leads the attack on the space gun: his name is Theotokopulos.

In the fiction published in John Campbell's *Astounding/Analog*, after its brief glory, success was equated with intelligence; Campbell once wrote that if a superman existed among us today he would be found at the head of a giant corporation.

Military officers, brave men under discipline, were considered the noblest form of human life. In a ritual gesture, the authors of these stories sneered at spoiled women and children, lazy welfare recipients, and cowardly bureaucrats who made life difficult for the hard and strong. These attitudes, too, have persisted.

Up until about 1950 there had always been one or two token women writers in science fiction; they were expected to accept their modest place and conform to masculine standards. Leigh Brackett, the most successful of them, wrote exclusively about macho males. She was fortunate in her first name, which could be taken as either F or M; Catherine L. Moore disguised her sex with initials.

It was understood that science fiction was intended for adolescent males, and as late as the sixties Lester del Rey told Kate Wilhelm very seriously that she ought to get out of the field because she was not providing heroic role-models for boys.

The first serious threat to John Campbell's domination of the field came in 1950, when H. L. Gold started the magazine *Galaxy*. Gold filled his early issues with stories by Theodore Sturgeon, Fritz Leiber, Isaac Asimov and others whom Campbell had considered his own.

Campbell's first response was petulant: he had *Astounding*'s cover redesigned to resemble that of *Galaxy*, as if to say, "If you can steal from me, I can steal from you."

His next was shrewder. Over the next decade, he deliberately cultivated technically oriented writers with marginal writing skills, who could not hope to sell to more discriminating editors. Surveys had already shown that a large percentage of *Astounding*'s readers were technically or scientifically trained: they were interested in ideas, and didn't care if the stories were well or badly written. Although he continued to compete with Gold (and Boucher) for established writers, Campbell was building a new stable that he knew he could keep. The separation between *Astounding* and all the other magazines was permanently restored.

A year before *Galaxy*, Anthony Boucher and J. Francis McComas had started *The Magazine of Fantasy*, later *The Magazine of Fantasy & Science Fiction*. It was never a direct threat to Campbell, or Gold either, but it was an equally important influence on the field because of its emphasis on polished and elegant prose.

Galaxy foundered and went down in 1980, but its work was done: *Isaac Asimov's* is its direct descendant. *Analog* and *F&SF* found their niches and are still here.

Horace Gold had overturned Campbell's empire, forced him into a strategic retreat, and changed the direction of science fiction in ways which are still felt. Gold attracted the strongest writers in the field because he could liberate them from the restraints Campbell had imposed: e.g., no hint of sexuality, no alien intelligences superior to homo sap's, no pessimism.

I know better than to claim that humane science fiction was invented in the fifties. It can be found in the Gernsback era. Jack Williamson published a story in *Wonder* in the early thirties about the anguish of an international team of scientists stranded on Mars when their countries go to war. But in the fifties this kind of compassionate, human-oriented science fiction became a dominant force.

Other magazines came and went like mayflies in the fifties. *Marvel Science Stories* briefly experimented with a blend of science fiction, sex, and sadism, along the lines of the horror pulps of the thirties. For some reason this did not work.

Planet Stories had a longer run; it published some interesting short pieces, including Ray Bradbury's, to add spice to its planetary diet. *If*, edited by Larry Shaw, was an ambitious magazine competing directly with *Galaxy*; it published, among other things, the novella that formed the first part of James Blish's novel *A Case of Conscience*.

After *Astounding*, *Galaxy*, and *F&SF*, the most successful and influential magazines of the fifties were *Thrilling Wonder* and *Startling Stories*, edited by Samuel Merwin, Jr. Merwin, who took over the two magazines in 1945, quickly tired of their juvenile antics, zapped the "Sergeant Saturn" letter column, and upgraded the magazines to a point about equidistant among the three leaders. He published a number of notable stories, including Philip José Farmer's "The Lovers," a story of human-insect miscegenation that none of the other editors would touch. Gold bounced that one, and it is unlikely that Boucher and McComas would have considered it: *F&SF* was a decorous magazine. Gold did buy and publish two landmark stories by Fritz Leiber that dealt with unorthodox or kinky sex: "Nice Girl With Five Husbands" and "Coming Attraction."

John Campbell told us in the introduction to his collection *Who Goes There?* that "Twilight," his first Don A. Stuart story, was rejected by every s.f. and fantasy magazine in existence at the time it was written: he was able to sell it only after *Astounding* changed publishers. I had a similar experience with "Not With a Bang."

At times when the number of magazine editors in the field has declined to three, a number which seems to represent its ground state, authors complain that good things go unpublished because they happen to collide with the prejudices of all three. Then a new editor comes along and scoops up all the rejected masterpieces, and for a while his magazine burns bright.

In his introduction to *Who Goes There?* Campbell wrote, "Basically, science-fiction is an effort to predict the future on the basis of known facts, culled largely from present-day science laboratories." He probably got this idea from Hugo Gernsback and from the "world of the future" enthusiasm generated by the 1939 World's Fair. And there was the example of Jules Verne's predictions: the submarine (which already existed), the periscope (which Verne never mentioned), the space gun (which wouldn't work).

Two pages later, Campbell had a second thought: "You can consider any social structure you like, carried to any extreme you need, to bring out your points. One thing, and one thing only, is properly demanded of the story, once its reasonable premise is set forth: the story must be self-consistent from there on."

In the introduction to *Cloak of Aesir*, his second story collection, he said, "Science-fiction can be, and by rights ought to be, philosophical in nature."

That's closer, but not close enough. Science fiction's predictive successes, as Heinlein has pointed out, are no more frequent than chance can account for; as a game, s.f. is fun but trivial; philosophically it is usually shallow, and yet there is something about science fiction that makes it important enough to keep us coming back to it. From my limited and biased viewpoint, it is the opportunity to use a premise, even an absurd premise, to perform an experiment which can't be carried out in the real world.

Campbell's son-in-law, Ian Robertson, told me a story about one of their conversations on a trip they took together. "I guess I must have used the word 'beautiful,' which was a dangerous thing; I mean anything was dangerous. 'Well,' he said, 'let me tell you something. Years ago, when I was around twelve, I was sitting in a peach orchard in New Jersey, and all the blossoms were out. I had the feeling that this was very beautiful, and I had to find out why. I finally decided, 'This is my world, and I belong in it. Without this world I couldn't physically exist. I'd damn well *better* think it's beautiful.' "

I have spent a good deal of time wondering what makes the difference between artists and other people. Isolation seems to have something to do with it, but sometimes the isolation is self-imposed. Writers and painters, mathematicians and inventors, composers and film-makers come in all shapes and sizes.

In the lobby of the airport in Bali three half-naked boys were carving a floor-to-ceiling slab of gray stone into an elaborate bas-relief of elephants, flowers, palm trees and birds. They were not more than nine or ten years old. They saw our astonishment and were amused. They went back to their carving.

A teacher we know, a former Clarion student, used the Clarion Workshop method in a sixth-grade writing class. Her pupils wrote poems; they wrote short stories; they wrote novels. The principal disallowed the prizes they won; he said they couldn't have done all that by themselves. The teacher asked them to do it again under observation. They did it again.

Is writing or art something we do against instruction? If so, what makes some of us stubborn enough to insist that milk is white?

I was primed to become a member of the s.f. revolution of the fifties. I could not write about firm-jawed outdoorsmen and their swooning sweethearts, because I had no personal experience of either. My resentment of injustice and my dislike of stupidity would not allow me to invent alien menaces who looked like Japs with green scales. My esthetic sense was offended by the clunky prose and mechanical construction of macho science fiction.

In "Double Meaning," indeed, I used a rather firm-jawed and ruthless viewpoint character, but I made him the villain, much as I took the hero of Hubbard's "To the Stars" and made him the villain of "The Earth Quarter."

The hero of "Double Meaning" is Jawj Pembun: he is a colonial, he is nonwhite, he is despised and patronized, and eventually he humbles his betters. The real hero of "Rule Golden" is Aza-Kra, the monster from outer space.

When Joe Haldeman reprinted "Rule Golden" in an anthology, he remarked that I had solved the problem of war by changing human nature. I think he missed the point. If by "human nature" we mean saps' tendency to violence, "Rule Golden" solves the problem not by changing human nature but by controlling it.

Every society already controls "human nature" by various means; they don't work perfectly, but they work, and that's why most adults (unlike small boys) can walk down the street without wondering if they are going to be assaulted by every larger contemporary male they see.

As it happens, neither of these novellas appeared in *Galaxy*. They were shaped by the market Gold created and probably would not have been written without him, but he rejected them both.

One of the strategies of ambitious short-story writers is to write novellas, in order to claim more of the available territory. One of the strategies of ambitious editors is to resist this tendency, in order to get more variety into their magazines and encourage more writers. "Double Meaning" was published in *Startling Stories*, edited by Sam Merwin; "Rule Golden" was published in Harry Harrison's *Science Fiction Adventures*.

Neither one could have appeared in *Astounding* at that time, because both of them broke the inferior-aliens rule. Arthur Clarke's "Guardian Angel," which he later expanded into the novel *Childhood's End*, could not be published there for the same reason; it appeared in *Famous Fantastic Mysteries*, edited by Mary Gnaedinger. (Isaac Asimov got around this problem by populating his galactic empire exclusively with human beings.) *Astounding* was full of dumb aliens, many of them entertainingly invented by Eric Frank Russell (whose moving "Dear Devil," about a wise and benevolent old Martian, could not be sold to Campbell; it appeared in *Other Worlds*, edited by Raymond A. Palmer).

It is worth asking why Campbell made this rule and enforced it adamantly, since he himself, as "Don A. Stuart," had made a career of breaking it in the late thirties (in *Astounding*, before he became editor).

I don't know the answer, but Campbell was a many-sided man. In the forties he adopted a persona that believed fervently in the Destiny of Man to Conquer the Universe, a megalomaniac credo that still reverberates in science fiction. I think he subscribed to the credo himself at that time, but I also think he sensed that it was just the ticket for young male readers who doubted their own puissance. And I think he was right.

When he created "Don A. Stuart" Campbell gave shape to one element of his personality. Another one appeared as "Karl van Campen," the author of a tongue-in-cheek story called "The Irrelevant" which excited controversy when it was published in *Astounding* in 1934.

Van Campen was the trickster, the wily debater ("slippery as an eel in oil," said John D. Clark), who frequently reasoned from jiggered premises to outlandish conclusions. It was van Campen who wrote most of Campbell's editorials: in one of these he argued persuasively against the validity of logical argument; in others he defended cancer-cure quacks, the manufacturer of Thalidomide, and racial discrimination.

I had other grievances against Campbell. In his restless urge to distance himself from the pack, he indulged in the fifties another persona, the credulous chela of pseudoscientists. One after another he trotted them out: Ehrenhaft, the discoverer of a nonexistent magnetic current; Dean, the inventor of an antigravity device which could not be produced for inspection; Hubbard, the founder of Dianetics and later head of the Church of Scientology; Hieronymous, the inventor of a "psionic" device that worked just as well when a wiring diagram was substituted for its electronic parts.

What bothered me was that when one of these fantasies was exploded, as when a reader pointed out the flaws in Campbell's suggestion that a submarine powered by a Dean machine could be flown to Mars tomorrow morning, he never admitted that he had been wrong but simply went on to the next nutty idea.

In the sixties, one morning in the shower, I composed a song about all this:

> Oh, the Dean Machine, the Dean Machine,
> You put it right in a submarine,
> And it flies so high that it can't be seen—
> The wonderful, wonderful Dean Machine!
>
> Oh, the therapy, the therapy,
> That Hubbard gave to JWC,
> And it took him back to his infancy—
> The wonderful, wonderful therapy!
>
> The magnetic flow, the magnetic flow
> That Ehrenhaft sold him so long ago,
> And he swore up and down it was really so—
> The wonderful, super magnetic flow!
>
> Oh, the psi folderol, the psi folderol,
> It never needs fixing, whatever befall,
> For there's nothing inside it at all, at all—
> The wonderful, wonderful psi folderol!

* * *

My first attempt to reform the world was in 1939, when I wrote an article called "Unite or Fie," advocating the formation of a national fan organization. Art Widner published the article in his fanzine, put the organization together—the National Fantasy Fan Federation—and served as its first president. I believe it still exists.

My next effort was the Milford Science Fiction Conference, which I founded with Judith Merril in 1956; then came Science Fiction Writers of America (SFWA), which I founded in 1965. More recently I have become the founder of the Committee of One to Get the *W* Out of "Wracked" (COGWOW), and the Contracts and Related Areas of Publishing Special Interest Group (crapSIG), which bestows on publishers its coveted Seal of Disapproval (SOD).

Almost forty years ago I worked for a publisher who fired seven people just before Christmas, in order to avoid paying their bonuses. Later, when the company was on the skids, he offered a senior editor the option of being let go immediately, with severance pay based on his current salary, or taking a lower-paying job. The editor took the job; then the publisher fired him and paid off at the lower rate. Unlike the next publisher I worked for, he was a handsome man, but I think he was a giant toad at heart. Long experience has made me tend to think of all publishers in these terms, although there are some brilliant exceptions.

As president of SFWA, to my deep satisfaction, I was able to bully Ace Books into giving up their pirated editions of the Tolkien trilogy and paying the author $9,000 in back royalties.

Meanwhile the same reformist impulse was expressing itself in fiction. I was trying to explore other ways of organizing society, and to demonstrate other ways of writing science fiction, just as Campbell had done in the thirties. I had good company in this enterprise: Theodore Sturgeon, Fritz Leiber, Algis Budrys, and Cyril Kornbluth.

I believe all of us had felt somehow betrayed by Campbell. With Gold's encouragement, we tried to revive the revolution Campbell had aborted a decade earlier—not just to make money in our profession, but to bring something beautiful and necessary into being.

RULE GOLDEN

I

A MAN IN DES MOINES KICKED HIS WIFE WHEN HER BACK
was turned. She was taken to the hospital, suffering from a
broken coccyx.

So was he.

In Kansas City, Kansas, a youth armed with a .22 killed
a schoolmate with one shot through the chest, and instantly
dropped dead of heart-failure.

In Decatur two middleweights named Packy Morris and
Leo Oshinsky simultaneously knocked each other out.

In St. Louis, a policeman shot down a fleeing bank robber and collapsed. The bank robber died; the policeman's
condition was described as critical.

I read those items in the afternoon editions of the Washington papers, and although I noted the pattern, I wasn't
much impressed. Every newspaperman knows that runs of
coincidence are a dime a dozen; *everything* happens that
way—plane crashes, hotel fires, suicide pacts, people running amok with rifles, people giving away all their money;
name it and I can show you an epidemic of it in the files.

What I was actually looking for were stories originating
in two places: my home town and Chillicothe, Missouri.

Stories with those datelines had been carefully cut out of the papers before I got them, so, for the lack of anything better, I read everything datelined near either place. And that was how I happened to catch the Des Moines, Kansas City, Decatur and St. Louis items—all of those places will fit into a two-hundred-mile circle drawn with Chillicothe as its center.

I had asked for, but hadn't got, a copy of my own paper. That made it a little tough, because I had to sit there, in a Washington hotel room at night—and if you know a lonelier place and time, tell me—and wonder if they had really shut us down.

I knew it was unlikely. I knew things hadn't got that bad in America yet, by a long way. I knew they *wanted* me to sit there and worry about it, but I couldn't help it.

Ever since *La Prensa*, every newspaper publisher on this continent has felt a cold wind blowing down his back.

That's foolishness, I told myself. Not to wave the flag too much or anything, but the free speech tradition in this country is too strong; we haven't forgotten Peter Zenger.

And then it occurred to me that a lot of editors must have felt the same way, just before their papers were suppressed on the orders of an American president named Abraham Lincoln.

So I took one more turn around the room and got back into bed, and although I had already read all the papers from bannerlines to box scores, I started leafing through them again, just to make a little noise. Nothing to do.

I had asked for a book, and hadn't got it. That made sense, too; there was nothing to do in that room, nothing to distract me, nothing to read except newspapers—and how could I look at a newspaper without thinking of the *Herald-Star*?

My father founded the *Herald-Star*—the *Herald* part, that is, the *Star* came later—ten years before I was born. I inherited it from him, but I want to add that I'm not one of those publishers by right of primogeniture whose only function consists in supplying sophomoric by-lined copy for the front page; I started on the paper as a copy boy and I can still handle any job in a city room.

It was a good newspaper. It wasn't the biggest paper in the Middle West, or the fastest growing, or the loudest; but we'd had two Pulitzer prizes in the last fifteen years, we kept our political bias on the editorial page, and up to now we had never knuckled under to anybody.

But this was the first time we had picked a fight with the U.S. Department of Defense.

Ten miles outside Chillicothe, Missouri, the Department had a little thousand-acre installation with three laboratory buildings, a small airfield, living quarters for a staff of two hundred and a one-story barrack. It was closed down in 1968 when the Phoenix-bomb program was officially abandoned.

Two years and ten months later, it was opened up again. A new and much bigger barrack went up in place of the old one; a two-company garrison moved in. Who else or what else went into the area, nobody knew for certain; but rumors came out.

We checked the rumors. We found confirmation. We published it, and we followed it up. Within a week we had a full-sized crusade started; we were asking for a congressional investigation, and it looked as if we might get it.

Then the President invited me and the publishers of twenty-odd other anti-administration dailies to Washington. Each of us got a personal interview with The Man; the Secretary of Defense was also present, to evade questions.

They asked me, as a personal favor and in the interests of national security, to kill the Chillicothe series.

After asking a few questions, to which I got the answers I expected, I politely declined.

And here I was.

The door opened. The guard outside looked in, saw me on the bed, and stepped back out of sight. Another man walked in: stocky build, straight black hair turning gray; about fifty. Confident eyes behind rimless bifocals.

"Mr. Dahl. My name is Carlton Frisbee."

"I've seen your picture," I told him. Frisbee was the Under Secretary of Defense, a career man, very able; he was said to be the brains of the Department.

He sat down facing me. He didn't ask permission, and he didn't offer to shake hands, which was intelligent of him.

"How do you feel about it now?" he asked.

"Just the same."

He nodded. After a moment he said, "I'm going to try to explain our position to you, Mr. Dahl."

I grinned at him. "The word you're groping for is 'awkward.' "

"No. It's true that we can't let you go in your present state of mind, but we can keep you. If necessary, you will be killed, Mr. Dahl. That's how important Chillicothe is."

"Nothing," I said, "is that important."

He cocked his head at me. "If you and your family lived in a community surrounded by hostile savages, who were kept at bay only because you had rifles—and if someone proposed to give them rifles—well?"

"Look," I said, "let's get down to cases. You claim that a new weapon is being developed at Chillicothe, is that right? It's something revolutionary, and if the Russians got it first we would be sunk, and so on. In other words, the Manhattan Project all over again."

"Right."

"Okay. Then why has Chillicothe got twice the military guard it had when it was an atomic research center, and a third of the civilian staff?"

He started to speak.

"Wait a minute, let me finish. Why, of the fifty-one scientists we have been able to trace to Chillicothe, are there seventeen linguists and philologists, three organic chemists, five physiologists, *twenty-six psychologists, and not one single physicist*?"

"In the first place—were you about to say something?"

"All right, go ahead."

"You know I can't answer those questions factually, Mr. Dahl, but speaking conjecturally, can't you conceive of a psychological weapon?"

"You can't answer them at all. My third question is, why have you got a wall around that place—not just a stockade, a wall, with guard towers on it? Never mind speaking conjecturally. Now I'll answer your question. Yes, I can conceive of psychological experimentation that you might call weapons research, I can think of several possibilities, and there isn't a damn one of them that wouldn't have to be used on American citizens before you could get anywhere near the Russians with it.''

His eyes were steady behind the bright lenses. He didn't say, ''We seem to have reached a deadlock,'' or ''Evidently it would be useless to discuss this any further''; he simply changed the subject.

''There are two things we can do with you, Mr. Dahl; the choice will be up to you. First, we can indict you for treason and transfer you to a Federal prison to await trial. Under the revised Alien and Sedition Act, we can hold you incommunicado for at least twelve months, and, of course, no bail will be set. I feel bound to point out to you that in this case, it would be impossible to let you come to trial until the danger of breaching security at Chillicothe is past. If necessary, as I told you, you would die in prison.

''Second, we can admit you to Chillicothe itself as a press representative. We would, in this case, allow you full access to all nontechnical information about the Chillicothe project as it develops, with permission to publish as soon as security is lifted. You would be confined to the project until that time, and I can't offer you any estimate of how long it might be. In return, you would be asked to write letters plausibly explaining your absence to your staff and to close friends and relatives, and—providing that you find Chillicothe to be what we say it is and not what you suspect—to work out a series of stories for your newspaper which will divert attention from the project.''

He seemed to be finished. I said, ''Frisbee, I hate to tell you this, but you're overlooking a point. Let's just suppose for a minute that Chillicothe is what I think it is. How do I know that once I got inside I might not somehow or other find myself writing that kind of copy whether I felt like it or not?''

He nodded. ''What guarantees would you consider sufficient?''

I thought about that. It was a nice point. I was angry enough, and scared enough, to feel like pasting Frisbee a

good one and then seeing how far I could get; but one thing
I couldn't figure out, and that was why, if Frisbee wasn't at
least partly on the level, he should be here at all.

If they wanted me in Chillicothe, they could drag me
there.

After a while I said, "Let me call my managing editor
and tell him where I'm going. Let me tell him that I'll call
him again—*on a video circuit*—within three days after I get
there, when I've had time to inspect the whole area. And
that if I don't call, or I look funny or sound funny, he can
start worrying."

He nodded again. "Fair enough." He stood up. "I won't
ask you to shake hands with me now, Mr. Dahl; later on I
hope you will." He turned and walked to the door, unhur-
ried, calm, imperturbable, the way he had come in.

Six hours later I was on a westbound plane.

That was the first day.

The second day, an inexplicable epidemic broke out in
the slaughterhouses of Chicago and surrounding areas. The
symptoms were a sudden collapse followed by nausea, in-
continence, anemia, shock, and in some cases, severe pain
in the occipital and cervical regions. Or: as one victim, an
A. F. of L. knacker with twenty-five years' experience in
the nation's abattoirs, succinctly put it: "It felt just like I
was hit in the head."

Local and Federal health authorities immediately closed
down the affected slaughterhouses, impounded or banned
the sale of all supplies of fresh meat in the area, and
launched a sweeping investigation. Retail food stores sold
out their stocks of canned, frozen and processed meats early
in the day; seafood markets reported their largest volume
of sales in two decades. Eggs and cheese were in short
supply.

Fifty-seven guards, assistant wardens and other minor officials of the Federal penitentiary at Leavenworth, Kansas,
submitted a group resignation to Warden Hermann R.
Longo. Their explanation of the move was that all had experienced a religious conversion, and that assisting in the

forcible confinement of other human beings was inconsonant with their beliefs.

Near Louisville, Kentucky, neighbors attracted by cries for help found a forty-year-old woman and her twelve-year-old daughter both severely burned. The woman, whose clothing was not even scorched although her upper body was covered with first and second degree burns, admitted pushing the child into a bonfire, but in her hysterical condition was unable to give a rational account of her own injuries.

There was also a follow-up on the Des Moines story about the man who kicked his wife. Remember that I didn't say he had a broken coccyx; I said he was suffering from one. A few hours after he was admitted to the hospital he stopped doing so, and he was released into police custody when X-rays showed no fracture.

Straws in the wind.

At five-thirty that morning, I was waking up my managing editor, Eli Freeman, with a monitored long-distance call—one of Frisbee's bright young men waiting to cut me off if I said anything I shouldn't. The temptation was strong, just the same, but I didn't.

From six to eight-thirty I was on a plane with three taciturn guards. I spent most of the time going over the last thirty years of my life, and wondering how many people would remember me two days after they wrapped my obituary around their garbage.

We landed at the airfield about a mile from the Project proper, and after one of my hitherto silent friends had finished a twenty-minute phone call, a limousine took us over to a long, temporary-looking frame building just outside the wall. It took me only until noon to get out again; I had been fingerprinted, photographed, stripped, examined, X-rayed, urinanalyzed, blood-tested, showered, disinfected, and given a set of pinks to wear until my own clothes had been cleaned and fumigated. I also got a numbered badge which I was instructed to wear on the left chest at all times, and an identity card to keep in my wallet when I got my wallet back.

Then they let me through the gate, and I saw Chillicothe.

I was in a short cul-de-sac formed by the gate and two
walls of masonry, blank except for firing slits. Facing away
from the gate I could see one of the three laboratory buildings a good half-mile away. Between me and it was a geo-
metrical forest of poles with down-pointing reflectors on
their crossbars. Floodlights.

I didn't like that. What I saw a few minutes later I liked
even less. I was bouncing across the flat in a jeep driven by
a stocky, moon-faced corporal; we passed the first building,
and I saw the second.

There was a ring of low pillboxes around it. And their
guns pointed *inward*, toward the building.

Major General Parst was a big, bald man in his fifties,
whose figure would have been more military if the Prussian
corset had not gone out of fashion. I took him for a Pentagon soldier; he had the Pentagon smoothness of manner,
but there seemed to be a good deal more under it than the
usual well-oiled vacancy. He was also, I judged, a very
worried man.

"There's just one thing I'd like to make clear to you at
the beginning, Mr. Dahl. I'm not a grudge-holding man,
and I hope you're not either, because there's a good chance
that you and I will be seeing a lot of each other during the
next three or four years. But I thought it might make it a
little easier for you to know that you're not the only one
with a grievance. You see this isn't an easy job, it never has
been. I'm just stating the fact: it's been considerably harder
since your newspaper took an interest in us." He spread his
hands and smiled wryly.

"Just what is your job, General?"

"You mean, what is Chillicothe." He snorted. "I'm not
going to waste my breath telling you."

My expression must have changed.

"Don't misunderstand me—I mean that if I told you, you
wouldn't believe me. I didn't myself. I'm going to have to
show you." He stood up, looking at his wristwatch. "I have
a little more than an hour. That's more than enough for the
demonstration, but you're going to have a lot of questions
afterward. We'd better start."

He thumbed his intercom. "I'll be in Section One for the next fifteen minutes."

When we were in the corridor outside he said, "Tell me something, Mr. Dahl: I suppose it occurred to you that if you were right in your suspicions of Chillicothe, you might be running a certain personal risk in coming here, in spite of any precautions you might take?"

"I considered the possibility. I haven't seen anything to rule it out yet."

"And still, I gather that you chose this alternative almost without hesitation. Why was that, if you don't mind telling me?"

It was a fair question. There's nothing very attractive about a Federal prison, but at least they don't saw your skull open there, or turn your mind inside out with drugs. I said, "Call it curiosity."

He nodded. "Yes. A very potent force, Mr. Dahl. More mountains have been moved by it than by faith."

We passed a guard with a T44, then a second, and a third. Finally Parst stopped at the first of two metal doors. There was a small pane of thick glass set into it at eye-level, and what looked like a microphone grill under that. Parst spoke into the grill: "Open up Three, Sergeant."

"Yes, sir."

I followed Parst to the second door. It slid open as we reached it and we walked into a large, empty room. The door closed behind us with a thud and a solid *click*. Both sounds rattled back startlingly; the room was solid metal, I realized—floor, walls and ceiling.

In the opposite wall was another heavy door. To my left was a huge metal hemisphere, painted the same gray as the walls, with a machine-gun's snout projecting through a horizontal slit in a deadly and impressive manner.

Echoes blurred the General's voice: "This is Section One. We're rather proud of it. The only entrance to the central room is here. The gun room is accessible only from the corridor outside."

He motioned me over to the other door. "This door is double," he said. "It's going to be an airlock eventually, we hope. All right, Sergeant."

The door slid back, exposing another one a yard farther in; like the others, it had a thick inset panel of glass.

Parst stepped in and waited for me. "Get ready for a shock," he said.

I loosened the muscles in my back and shoulders; my wind isn't what it used to be, but I can still hit. *Get ready for one yourself,* I thought, *if this is what I think it is.*

I walked into the tiny room, and heard the door thump behind me. Parst motioned to the glass pane.

I saw a room the size of the one behind me. There was a washbasin in it, and a toilet, and what looked like a hammock slung across one corner, and a wooden table with papers and a couple of pencils or crayons on it.

And against the far wall, propped upright on an ordinary lunch-counter stool, was something I couldn't recognize at all; I saw it and I didn't see it. If I had looked away then, I couldn't possibly have told anyone what it looked like.

Then it stirred slightly, and I realized that it was alive.

I saw that it had eyes.

I saw that it had arms.

I saw that it had legs.

Very gradually the rest of it came into focus. The top was about four feet off the floor, a small truncated cone about the size and shape of one of those cones of string that merchants used to keep to tie packages. Under that came the eyes, three of them. They were round and oyster-gray, with round black pupils, and they faced in different directions. They were set into a flattened bulb of flesh that just fitted under the base of the cone; there was no nose, no ears, no mouth, and no room for any.

The cone was black; the rest of the thing was a very dark, shiny blue-gray.

The head, if that is the word, was supported by a thin neck from which a sparse growth of fuzzy spines curved down and outward, like a botched attempt at feathers. The neck thickened gradually until it became the torso. The torso was shaped something like a bottle gourd, except that the upper lobe was almost as large as the lower. The upper lobe expanded and contracted evenly, all around, as the thing breathed.

Between each arm and the next, the torso curved inward to form a deep vertical gash.

There were three arms and three legs, spaced evenly around the body so that you couldn't tell front from back. The arms sprouted just below the top of the torso, the legs from its base. The legs were bent only slightly to reach the floor; each hand, with five slender, shapeless fingers, rested on the opposite-number thigh. The feet were a little like a chicken's . . .

I turned away and saw Parst; I had forgotten he was there, and where I was, and who I was. I don't recall planning to say anything, but I heard my own voice, faint and hoarse: "Did you *make* that?"

II

"STOP IT!" HE SAID SHARPLY.

I was trembling. I had fallen into a crouch without realizing it, weight on my toes, fists clenched.

I straightened up slowly and put my hands into my pockets. "Sorry."

The speaker rasped.

"Is everything all right, sir?"

"Yes, Sergeant," said Parst. "We're coming out." He turned as the door opened, and I followed him, feeling all churned up inside.

Halfway down the corridor I stopped. Parst turned and looked at me.

"Ithaca," I said.

Five months back there had been a Monster-from-Mars scare in and around Ithaca, New York; several hundred people had seen, or claimed to have seen, a white wingless aircraft hovering over various out-of-the-way places; and over thirty, including one very respectable Cornell professor, had caught sight of something that wasn't a man in the woods around Cayuga Lake. None of these people had got close enough for a good look, but nearly all of them agreed on one point—the thing walked erect, but had too many arms and legs. . . .

"Yes," said Parst. "That's right. But let's talk about it in my office, Mr. Dahl."

I followed him back there. As soon as the door was shut I said, "Where did it come from? Are there any more of them? What about the ship?"

He offered me a cigarette. I took it and sat down, hitting the chair by luck.

"Those are just three of the questions we can't answer," he said. "He claims that his home world revolves around a sun in our constellation of Aquarius; he says that it isn't visible from Earth. He also—"

I said, "He talks—? You've taught him to speak English?" For some reason that was hard to accept; then I remembered the linguists.

"Yes. Quite well, considering that he doesn't have vocal cords like ours. He uses a tympanum under each of those vertical openings in his body—those are his mouths. His name is Aza-Kra, by the way. I was going to say that he also claims to have come here alone. As for the ship, he says it's hidden, but he won't tell us where. We've been searching that area, particularly the hills near Cayuga and the lake itself, but we haven't turned it up yet. It's been suggested that he may have launched it under remote control and put it into an orbit somewhere outside the atmosphere. The Lunar Observatory is watching for it, and so are the orbital stations, but I'm inclined to think that's a dead end. In any case, that's not my responsibility. He had some gadgets in his possession when he was captured, but even those are being studied elsewhere. Chillicothe is what you saw a few minutes ago, and that's all it is. God knows it's enough."

His intercom buzzed. "Yes."

"Dr. Meshevski would like to talk to you about the technical vocabularies, sir."

"Ask him to hold it until the conference if he possibly can."

"Yes, sir."

"Two more questions we can't answer," Parst said, "are

what his civilization is like and what he came here to do. I'll tell you what he says. The planet he comes from belongs to a galactic union of highly advanced, peace-loving races. He came here to help us prepare ourselves for membership in that union."

I was trying hard to keep up, but it wasn't easy. After a moment I said, "Suppose it's true?"

He gave me the cold eye.

"All right, suppose it's true." For the first time, his voice was impatient. "Then suppose the opposite. Think about it for a minute."

I saw where he was leading me, but I tried to circle around to it from another direction; I wanted to reason it out for myself. I couldn't make the grade; I had to fall back on analogies, which are a kind of thinking I distrust.

You were a cannibal islander, and a missionary came along. He meant well, but you thought he wanted to steal your yamfields and your wives, so you chopped him up and ate him for dinner.

Or:

You were a cannibal islander, and a missionary came along. You treated him as a guest, but he made a slave of you, worked you till you dropped, and finally wiped out your whole nation, to the last woman and child.

I said, "A while ago you mentioned three or four years as the possible term of the Project. Did you—?"

"That wasn't meant to be taken literally," he said. "It may take a lifetime." He was staring at his desk-top.

"In other words, if nothing stops you, you're going to go right on just this way, sitting on this thing. Until What's-his-name dies, or his friends show up with an army, or something else blows it wide open."

"*That's* right."

"Well, damn it, don't you see that's the one thing you can't do? Either way you guess it, that won't work. If he's friendly—"

Parst lifted a pencil in his hand and slapped it palm-down against the desk-top. His mouth was tight. "It's *necessary*," he said.

After a silent moment he straightened in his chair and

spread the fingers of his right hand at me. "One," he said, touching the thumb: "weapons. Leaving everything else aside, if we can get one strategically superior weapon out of him, or the theory that will enable us to build one, then we've *got* to do it and we've *got* to do it in secret."

The index finger. "Two: the spaceship." Middle finger. "Three: the civilization he comes from. If they're planning to attack us we've got to find that out, and when, and how, and what we can do about it." Ring finger. "Four: Aza-Kra himself. If we don't hold him in secret we can't hold him at all, and how do we know what he might do if we let him go? There isn't a single possibility we can rule out. Not one."

He put the hand flat on the desk. "Five, six, seven, eight, nine, ten, infinity. Biology, psychology, sociology, ecology, chemistry, physics, right down the line. Every science. In any one of them we might find something that would mean the difference between life and death for this country or this whole planet."

He stared at me for a moment, his face set. "You don't have to remind me of the other possibilities, Dahl. I know what they are; I've been on this project for thirteen weeks. I've also heard of the Golden Rule, and the Ten Commandments, and the Constitution of the United States. But this is *the survival of the human race* we're talking about."

I opened my mouth to say "That's just the point," or something equally stale, but I shut it again; I saw it was no good. I had one argument—that if this alien ambassador was what he claimed to be, then the whole world had to know about it; any nation that tried to suppress that knowledge, or dictate the whole planet's future, was committing a crime against humanity. That, on the other hand, if he was an advance agent for an invasion fleet, the same thing was true only a great deal more so.

Beyond that I had nothing but instinctive moral conviction; and Parst had that on his side too; so did Frisbee and the President and all the rest. Being who and what they were, they had to believe as they did. Maybe they were right.

Half an hour later, the last thought I had before my head

hit the pillow was, *Suppose there isn't any Aza-Kra? Suppose that thing was a fake, a mechanical dummy?*

But I knew better, and I slept soundly.

That was the second day. On the third day, the front pages of the more excitable newspapers were top-heavy with forty-eight-point headlines. There were two Chicago stories. The first, in the morning editions, announced that every epidemic victim had made a complete recovery, that health department experts had been unable to isolate any disease-causing agent in the stock awaiting slaughter, and that although several cases not involving stockyard employees had been reported, not one had been traced to consumption of infected meat. A Chicago epidemiologist was quoted as saying. "It could have been just a gigantic coincidence."

The later story was a lulu. Although the slaughter-houses had not been officially reopened or the ban on fresh-meat sales rescinded, health officials allowed seventy of the previous day's victims to return to work as an experiment. Within half an hour every one of them was back in the hospital, suffering from a second, identical attack.

Oddly enough—at first glance—sales of fresh meat in areas outside the ban dropped slightly in the early part of the day ("They *say* it's all right, but you won't catch me taking a chance"), rose sharply in the evening ("I'd better stock up before there's a run on the butcher shops").

Warden Longo, in an unprecedented move, added his resignation to those of the fifty-seven "conscience" employees of Leavenworth. Well-known as an advocate of prison reform, Longo explained that his subordinates' example had convinced him that only so dramatic a gesture could focus the American public's attention upon the injustice and inhumanity of the present system.

He was joined by two hundred and three of the Federal institution's remaining employees, bringing the total to more than eighty per cent of Leavenworth's permanent staff.

The movement was spreading. In Terre Haute, Indiana, eighty employees of the Federal penitentiary were reported to have resigned. Similar reports came from the State prisons of Iowa, Missouri, Illinois and Indiana, and from city and county correctional institutions from Kansas City to Cincinnati.

The war in Indo-China was crowded back among the stock-market reports. Even the official announcement that the first Mars rocket was nearing completion in its sub-lunar orbit—front-page news at any normal time—got an inconspicuous paragraph in some papers and was dropped entirely by others.

But I found an item in a St. Louis paper about the policeman who had collapsed after shooting a criminal. He was dead.

I woke up a little before dawn that morning, having had a solid fifteen hours' sleep. I found the cafeteria and hung around until it opened. That was where Captain Ritchy-loo tracked me down.

He came in as I was finishing my second order of ham and eggs, a big, blond, swimming-star type, full of confidence and good cheer. "You must be Mr. Dahl. My name is Ritchy-loo."

I let him pump my hand and watched him sit down. "How do you spell it?" I asked him.

He grinned happily. "It is a tough one, isn't it? French. R,i,c,h,e,l,i,e,u."

Ritchy-loo.

I said, "What can I do for you, Captain?"

"Ah, it's what I can do for *you*, Mr. Dahl. You're a VIP around here, you know. You're getting the triple-A guided tour, and I'm your guide."

I *hate* people who are cheerful in the morning.

We went out into the pale glitter of early-morning sunshine on the flat; the floodlight poles and the pillboxes trailed long, mournful shadows. There was a jeep waiting, and Ritchy-loo took the wheel himself.

We made a right turn around the corner of the building and then headed down one of the diagonal avenues between the poles. I glanced into the firing slit of one of the pillboxes as we passed it, and saw the gleam of somebody's spectacles.

"That was B building that we just came out of," said the captain. "Most of the interesting stuff is there, but you want to see everything, naturally, so we'll go over to C first and then back to A.''

The huge barrack, far off to the right, looked deserted; I saw a few men in fatigues here and there, spearing stray bits of paper. Beyond the building we were heading for, almost against the wall, tiny figures were leaping rhythmically, opening and closing like so many animated scissors.

It was a well-policed area, at any rate; I watched for a while, out of curiosity, and didn't see a single cigarette paper or gum wrapper.

To the left of the barrack and behind it was a miniature town—neat one-story cottages, all alike, all the same distance apart. The thing that struck me about it was that there were none of the signs of a permanent camp—no borders of whitewashed stones, no trees, no shrubs, no flowers. *No wives*, I thought.

''How's morale here, Captain?'' I asked.

''Now, it's funny you should ask that. That happens to be my job, I'm the Company B morale officer. Well, I should say that all things considered, we aren't doing too badly. Of course, we have a few difficulties. These men are here on eighteen-month assignments, and that's kind of a long time without passes or furloughs. We'd like to make the hitches shorter, naturally, but of course you understand that there aren't too many fresh but seasoned troops available just now.''

''No.''

''*But*, we do our best. Now here's C building.''

Most of C building turned out to be occupied by chemical laboratories: long rows of benches covered by rank growths of glassware, only about a fifth of it working, and nobody watching more than a quarter of that.

''What are they doing here?''

''Over my head,'' said Ritchy-loo cheerfully. ''Here's Dr. Vitale, let's ask him.''

Vitale was a little sharp-featured man with a nervous blink. ''This is the atmosphere section,'' he said. ''We're trying to analyze the atmosphere which the alien breathes. Eventually we hope to manufacture it.''

That was a point that hadn't occurred to me. "He can't breathe our air?"

"No, no. Altogether different."

"Well, where does he get the stuff he does breathe, then?"

The little man's lips worked. "From that cone-shaped mechanism on the top of his head. An atmosphere plant that you could put in your pocket. Completely incredible. We can't get an adequate sample without taking it off him, and we can't take it off him without killing him. We have to deduce what he breathes in from what he breathes *out*. *Very* difficult." He went away.

All the same, I couldn't see much point in it. Presumably if Aza-Kra couldn't breathe our air, we couldn't breathe his—so anybody who wanted to examine him would have to wear an oxygen tank and a breathing mask.

But it was obvious enough, and I got it in another minute. If the prisoner didn't have his own air-supply, it would be that much harder for him to break out past the gun room and the guards in the corridors and the pillboxes and the floodlights and the wall. . . .

We went on, stopping at every door. There were storerooms, sleeping quarters, a few offices. The rest of the rooms were empty.

Ritchy-loo wanted to go on to A building, but I was being perversely thorough, and I said we would go through the barrack and the company towns first. We did; it took us three hours and thinned down Ritchy-loo's stream of cheerful conversation to a trickle. We looked everywhere, and of course we did not find anything that shouldn't have been there.

A building was the recreation hall. Canteen, library, gymnasium, movie theater, PX, swimming pool. It was also the project hospital and dispensary. Both sections were well filled.

So we went back to B. And it was almost noon, so we had lunch in the big air-conditioned cafeteria. I didn't look forward to it; I expected that rest and food would turn on Ritchy-loo's conversational spigot again, and if he didn't get any response to the first three or four general topics he tried,

I was perfectly sure he would begin telling me jokes. Nothing of the kind happened. After a few minutes I saw why, or thought I did. Looking around the room, I saw face after face with the same blank look on it; there wasn't a smile or an animated expression in the place. And now that I was paying attention I noticed that the sounds were odd, too. There were more than a hundred people in the room, enough to set up a beehive roar; but there was so little talking going on that you could pick out individual sentences with ease, and they were all trochaic—*Want* some *su*gar? *No*, thanks. Like that.

It was infectious; I was beginning to feel it now myself— an execution-chamber kind of mood, a feeling that we were all shut up in a place that we couldn't get out of, and where something horrible was going to happen. Unless you've ever been in a group made up of people who had that feeling and were reinforcing it in each other, it's indescribable; but it was very real and very hard to take.

Ritchy-loo left half a chop on his plate; I finished mine, but it choked me.

In the corridor outside I asked him, "Is it always as bad as that?"

"You noticed it too? That place gives me the creeps, I don't know why. It's the same way in the movies, too, lately—wherever you get a lot of these people together. I just don't understand it." For a second longer he looked worried and thoughtful, and then he grinned suddenly. "I don't want to say anything against civilians, Mr. Dahl, but I think that bunch is pretty far gone."

I could have hugged him. Civilians! If Ritchy-loo was more than six months away from a summer-camp counselor's job, I was a five-star general.

We started at the end of the corridor and worked our way down. We looked into a room with an X-ray machine and a fluoroscope in it, and a darkroom, and a room full of racks and filing cabinets, and a long row of offices.

Then Ritchy-loo opened a door that revealed two men standing on opposite sides of a desk, spouting angry German at each other. The tall one noticed us after a second, said, " 'St, 'st," to the other, and then to us, coldly, "You might, at least, knock."

"Sorry, gentlemen," said Ritchy-loo brightly. He closed the door and went on to the next on the same side. This opened onto a small, bare room with nobody in it but a stocky man with corporal's stripes on his sleeve. He was sitting hunched over, elbows on knees, hands over his face. He didn't move or look up.

I have a good ear, and I had managed to catch one sentence of what the fat man next door had been saying to the tall one. It went like this: *"Nein, nein, das ist bestimmt nicht die Klaustrophobie; Ich sage dir, es ist das dreifüssige Tier, das sie störrt."*

My college German came back to me when I prodded it, but it creaked a little. While I was still working at it, I asked Ritchy-loo, "What was that?"

"Psychiatric section," he said.

"You get many psycho cases here?"

"Oh, no," he said. "Just the normal percentage, Mr. Dahl. Less, in fact."

The captain was a poor liar.

"Klaustrophobie" was easy, of course. *"Dreifüssige Tier"* stopped me until I remembered that the German for "zoo" is *"Tiergarten."* *Dreifüssige Tier*: the three-footed beast. The triped.

The fat one had been saying to the tall one, "No, no, it is absolutely not claustrophobia; I tell you, it's the triped that's disturbing them."

Three-quarters of an hour later we had peered into the last room in B building: a long office full of IBM machines. We had now been over every square yard of Chillicothe, and I had seen for myself that no skulduggery was going forward anywhere in it. That was the idea behind the guided tour, as Ritchy-loo was evidently aware. He said, "Well, that just about wraps it up, Mr. Dahl. By the way, the General's office asked me to tell you that if it's all right with you, they'll set up that phone call for you for four o'clock this afternoon."

I looked down at the rough map of the building I'd been

drawing as we went along. "There's one place we haven't been, Captain," I said. "Section One."

"Oh, well that's right, that's right. You saw that yesterday, though, didn't you, Mr. Dahl?"

"For about two minutes. I wasn't able to take much of it in. I'd like to see it again, if it isn't too much trouble. Or even if it is."

Ritchy-loo laughed heartily. "Good enough. Just wait a second, I'll see if I can get you a clearance on it." He walked down the corridor to the nearest wall phone.

After a few moments he beckoned me over, palming the receiver. "The General says there are two research groups in there now and it would be a little crowded. He says he'd like you to postpone it if you think you can."

"Tell him that's perfectly all right, but in that case I think we'd better put off the phone call, too."

He repeated the message, and waited. Finally, "Yes. Yes, uh-huh. Yes, I've got that. All right."

He turned to me, "The general says it's all right for you to go in for half an hour and watch, but he'd appreciate it if you'll be careful not to distract the people who're working in there."

I had been hoping the General would say no. I wanted to see the alien again, all right, but what I wanted the most was time.

This was the second day I had been at Chillicothe. By tomorrow at the latest I would have to talk to Eli Freeman; and I still hadn't figured out any sure, safe way to tell him that Chillicothe was a legitimate research project, not to be sniped at by the *Herald-Star*—and make him understand that I didn't mean a word of it.

I could simply refuse to make the call, or I could tell him as much of the truth as I could before I was cut off—two words, probably—but it was a cinch that call would be monitored at the other end, too; that was part of what Ritchy-loo meant by "setting up the call." Somebody from the FBI would be sitting at Freeman's elbow . . . and I wasn't telling myself fairy tales about Peter Zenger any more.

They would shut the paper down, which was not only the

thing I wanted least in the world but a thing that would do nobody any good.

I wanted Eli to spread the story by underground channels—spread it so far, and time the release so well, that no amount of censorship could kill it.

Treason is a word every man has to define for himself.

Ritchy-loo did the honors for me at the gun room door, and then left me, looking a little envious. I don't think he had ever been inside Section One.

There was somebody ahead of me in the tiny antechamber, I found: a short, wide-shouldered man with a sheepdog tangle of black hair.

He turned as the door closed behind me. "Hi. Oh—you're Dahl, aren't you?" He had a young, pleasant, meaningless face behind dark-rimmed glasses. I said yes.

He put a half-inch of cigarette between his lips and shook hands with me. "Somebody pointed you out. Glad to know you; my name's Donnelly. Physical psych section—very junior." He pointed through the spy-window. "What do you think of him?"

Aza-Kra was sitting directly in front of the window; his lunch-counter stool had been moved into the center of the room. Around him were four men: two on the left, sitting on folding chairs, talking to him and occasionally making notes; two on the right, standing beside a waist-high enclosed mechanism from which wires led to the upper lobe of the alien's body. The ends of the wires were taped against his skin.

"That isn't an easy question," I said.

Donnelly nodded without interest. "That's my boss there," he said, "the skinny, gray-haired guy on the right. We get on each other's nerves. If he gets that setup operating this session, I'm supposed to go in and take notes. He won't, though."

"What is it?"

"Electroencephalograph. See, his brain isn't in his head, it's in his upper thorax there. Too much insulation in the way. We can't get close enough for a good reading without surgery. I say we ought to drop it till we get permission, but Hendricks thinks he can lick it. Those two on the other side are interviewers. Like to hear what they're saying?''

He punched one of two buttons set into the door beside the speaker grill, under the spy-window. ''If you're ever in here alone, remember you can't get out while this is on. You turn on the speaker here, it turns off the one in the gun room. They wouldn't be able to hear you ask to get out.''

Inside, a monotonous voice was saying, ''. . . have that here, but what exactly do you mean by . . .''

''I ought to be in physiology,'' Donnelly said, lowering his voice. ''They have all the fun. You see his eyes?''

I looked. The center one was staring directly toward us; the other two were tilted, almost out of sight around the curve of that bulb of blue-gray flesh.

''. . . in other words, just what is the nature of this energy, is it—uh—transmitted by waves, or . . .''

''He can look three ways at once,'' I said.

''Three, with binocular,'' Donnelly agreed. ''Each eye can function independently or couple with the one on either side. So he can have a series of overlapping monocular images, all the way around, or he can have up to three binocular images. They focus independently, too. He could read a newspaper and watch for his wife to come out of the movie across the street.''

''Wait a minute,'' I said. ''He has *six* eyes, not three?''

''Sure. Has to, to keep the symmetry and still get binocular vision.''

''Then he hasn't got any front or back,'' I said slowly.

''No, that's right. He's trilaterally symmetrical. Drive you crazy to watch him walk. His legs work the same way as his eyes—any one can pair up with either of the others. He wants to change direction, he doesn't have to turn around. I'd hate to try to catch him in an open field.''

''How did they catch him?'' I asked.

''Luckiest thing in the world. Found him in the woods with two broken ankles. Now look at his hands. What do you see?''

The voice inside was still droning; evidently it was a long question. ''Five fingers,'' I said.

''Nope.'' Donnelly grinned. ''One finger, four thumbs.

See how they oppose, those two on either side of the middle finger? He's got a better hand than ours. One *hell* of an efficient design. Brain in his thorax where it's safe, six eyes on a stalk—trachea up there too, no connection with the esophagus, so he doesn't need an epiglottis. Three of everything else. He can lose a leg and still walk, lose an arm and still type, lose two eyes and still see better than we do. He can lose—"

I didn't hear him. The interviewer's voice had stopped, and Aza-Kra's had begun. It was frightening, because it was a buzzing and it was a voice.

I couldn't take in a word of it; I had enough to do absorbing the fact that there were words.

Then it stopped, and the interviewer's ordinary, flat Middle Western voice began again.

"—And just try to sneak up behind him," said Donnelly.

Again Aza-Kra spoke briefly, and this time I saw the flesh at the side of his body, where the two lobes flowed together, bulge slightly and then relax.

"He's talking with one of his mouths," I said. "I mean, one of those—" I took a deep breath. "If he breathes through the top of his head, and there's no connection between his lungs and his vocal organs, then where the hell does he get the air?"

"He belches. Not as inconvenient as it sounds. You could learn to do it if you had to." Donnelly laughed. "Not very fragrant, though. Watch their faces when he talks."

I watched Aza-Kra's instead—what there was of it: one round, expressionless, oyster-colored eye staring back at me. With a human opponent, I was thinking, there were a thousand little things that you relied on to help you: facial expressions, mannerisms, signs of emotion. But Parst had been right when he said, *There isn't a single possibility we can rule out. Not one.* And so had the fat man: *It's the triped that's disturbing them.* And Ritchy-loo: *It's the same way . . . wherever you get a lot of these people together.*

And I still hadn't figured out any way to tell Freeman what he had to know.

I thought I could arouse Eli's suspicion easily enough; we

knew each other well enough for a word or a gesture to mean a good deal. I could make him look for hidden meanings. But how could I hide a message so that Eli would be more likely to dig it out than a trained FBI cryptologist?

I stared at Aza-Kra's glassy eye as if the answer were there. It was going to be a video circuit, I told myself. Donnelly was still yattering in my ear, and now the alien was buzzing again, but I ignored them both. Suppose I broke the message up into one-word units, scattered them through my conversation with Eli, and marked them off somehow—by twitching a finger, or blinking my eyelids?

A dark membrane flicked across the alien's oyster-colored eye.

A moment later, it happened again.

Donnelly was saying, ". . . intercostal membranes, apparently. But there's no trace of . . ."

"Shut up a minute, will you?" I said. "I want to hear this."

The inhuman voice, the voice that sounded like the articulate buzzing of a giant insect, was saying, "Comparison not possible, excuse me. If *(blink)* you try to understand in words you know, you *(blink)* tell yourself you wish *(blink)* to understand, but knowledge escape *(blink)* you. Can only show *(blink)* you from beginning, one *(blink)* little, another little. Not possible to carry all knowledge in one hand *(blink)*."

If you wish escape, show one hand.

I looked at Donnelly. He had moved back from the spy-window; he was lighting a cigarette, frowning at the match-flame. His mouth was sullen.

I put my left hand flat against the window. I thought, *I'm dreaming.*

The interviewer said querulously, ". . . getting us nowhere. Can't you—"

"Wait," said the buzzing voice. "Let me say, please. Ignorant man hold *(blink)* burning stick, say, this is breath *(blink)* of the wood. Then you show him flashlight—"

I took a deep breath, and held it.

Around the alien, four men went down together, folding

over quietly at waist and knee, sprawling on the floor. I heard a thump behind me.

Donnelly was lying stretched out along the wall, his head tilted against the corner. The cigarette had fallen from his hand.

I looked back at Aza-Kra. His head turned slightly, the dark flesh crinkling. Two eyes stared back at me through the window.

"Now you can breathe," said the monster.

III

I LET OUT THE BREATH THAT WAS CHOKING ME AND TOOK another. My knees were shaking.

"What did you do to them?"

"Put them to sleep only. In a few minutes I will put the others to sleep. After you are outside the doors. First we will talk."

I glanced at Donnelly again. His mouth was ajar; I could see his lips fluttering as he breathed.

"All right," I said, "talk."

"When you leave," buzzed the voice, "you must take me with you."

Now it was clear. He could put people to sleep, but he couldn't open locked doors. He had to have help.

"No deal," I said. "You might as well knock me out, too."

"Yes," he answered, "you will do it. When you understand."

"I'm listening."

"You do not have to agree now. I ask only this much. When we are finished talking, you leave. When you are past the second door, hold your breath again. Then go to the office of General Parst. You will find there papers about me. Read them. You will find also keys to open gun room. Also, handcuffs. Special handcuffs, made to fit me. Then you will think, if Aza-Kra is not what he says, would he agree to this? Then you will come back to gun room, use controls there to open middle door. You will lay handcuffs down, where you stand now, then go back to gun room, open inside door. I will put on the handcuffs. You will see that I do it. And then you will take me with you.''

. . . I said, ''Let me think.''

The obvious thing to do was to push the little button that turned on the audio circuit to the gun room, and yell for help; the alien could then put everybody to sleep from here to the wall, maybe, but it wouldn't do any good. Sooner or later he would have to let up, or starve to death along with the rest of us. On the other hand if I did what he asked— *anything* he asked—and it turned out to be the wrong thing, I would be guilty of the worst crime since Pilate's.

But I thought about it, I went over it again and again, and I couldn't see any loophole in it for Aza-Kra. He was leaving it up to me—if I felt like letting him out after I'd seen the papers in Parst's office, I could do so. If I didn't, I could still yell for help. In fact, I could get on the phone and yell to Washington, which would be a hell of a lot more to the point.

So where was the payoff for Aza-Kra? What was in those papers?

I pushed the button. I said, ''This is Dahl. Let me out, will you please?''

The outer door began to slide back. Just in time, I saw Donnelly's head bobbing against it; I grabbed him by the shirt-front and hoisted his limp body out of the way.

I walked across the echoing outer chamber; the outermost door opened for me. I stepped through it and held my breath. Down the corridor, three guards leaned over their rifles and toppled all in a row, like precision divers. Beyond them a hurrying civilian in the cross-corridor fell heavily and skidded out of sight.

The clacking of typewriters from a nearby office had

stopped abruptly. I let out my breath when I couldn't hold
it any longer, and listened to the silence.

The General was slumped over his desk, head on his
crossed forearms, looking pretty old and tired with his polished bald skull shining under the light. There was a faint
silvery scar running across the top of his head, and I wondered whether he had got it in combat as a young man, or
whether he had tripped over a rug at an embassy reception.

Across the desk from him a thin man in a gray pin-check
suit was jackknifed on the carpet, half-supported by a chair
leg, rump higher than his head.

There were two six-foot filing cabinets in the right-hand
corner behind the desk. Both were locked; the drawers of
the first one were labeled alphabetically, the other was un-
marked.

I unhooked Parst's keychain from his belt. He had as
many keys as a janitor or a high-school principal, but not
many of them were small enough to fit the filing cabinets.
I got the second one unlocked and began going through the
drawers. I found what I wanted in the top one—seven fat
manila folders labeled "Aza-Kra—Armor," "Aza-Kra—
General information," "Aza-Kra—Power sources," "Aza-
Kra—Spaceflight" and so on; and one more labeled
"Directives and related correspondence."

I hauled them all out, piled them on Parst's desk and
pulled up a chair.

I took "Armor" first because it was on top and because
the title puzzled me. The folder was full of transcripts of
interviews whose subject I had to work out as I went along.
It appeared that when captured, Aza-Kra had been wearing
a lightweight bulletproof armor, made of something that
was longitudinally flexible and perpendicularly rigid—in
other words, you could pull it on like a suit of winter un-
derwear, but you couldn't dent it with a sledge hammer.

They had been trying to find out what the stuff was and
how it was made for almost three months and as far as I
could see they had not made a nickel's worth of progress.

I looked through "Power sources" and "Spaceflight" to
see if they were the same, and they were. The odd part was
that Aza-Kra's answers didn't sound reluctant or evasive;

but he kept running into ideas for which there weren't any words in English and then they would have to start all over again, like Twenty Questions. . . . Is it animal? vegetable? mineral? It was a mess.

I put them all aside except "General information" and "Directives." The first, as I had guessed, was a catch-all for nontechnical subjects—where Aza-Kra had come from, what his people were like, his reasons for coming to this planet: all the unimportant questions; or the only questions that had any importance, depending on how you looked at it.

Parst had already given me an accurate summary of it, but it was surprisingly effective in Aza-Kra's words. *You say we want your planet. There are many planets, so many you would not believe. But if we wanted your planet, and if we could kill as you do, please understand, we are very many. We would fall on your planet like snowflakes. We would not send one man alone.*

And later: *Most young peoples kill. It is a law of nature, yes, but try to understand, it is not the only law. You have been a young people, but now you are growing older. Now you must learn the other law, not to kill. That is what I have come to teach. Until you learn this, we cannot have you among us.*

There was nothing in the folder dated later than a month and a half ago. They had dropped that line of questioning early.

The first thing I saw in the other folder began like this:

You are hereby directed to hold yourself in readiness to destroy the subject under any of the following circumstances, without further specific notification:

1, a: If the subject attempts to escape.

1, b: If the subject kills or injures a human being.

1, c: If the landing, anywhere in the world, of other members of the subject's race is reported and their similarity to the subject established beyond a reasonable doubt. . . .

Seeing it written down like that, in the cold dead-aliveness of black words on white paper, it was easy to forget that the alien was a stomach-turning monstrosity, and to see only that what he had to say was lucid and noble.

But I still hadn't found anything that would persuade me to help him escape. The problem was still there, as insoluble as ever. There was no way of evaluating a word the alien said about himself. He had come alone—perhaps—instead of bringing an invading army with him; but how did we know that one member of his race wasn't as dangerous to us as Perry's battleship to the Japanese? He might be; there was some evidence that he was.

My quarrel with the Defense Department was not that they were mistreating an innocent three-legged missionary, but simply that the problem of Aza-Kra belonged to the world, not to a fragment of the executive branch of the Government of the United States—and certainly not to me.

. . . There was one other way out, I realized. Instead of calling Frisbee in Washington, I could call an arm-long list of senators and representatives. I could call the UN secretariat in New York; I could call the editor of every major newspaper in this hemisphere and the head of every wire service and broadcasting chain. I could stir up a hornet's nest, even, as the saying goes, if I swung for it.

Wrong again: I couldn't. I opened the "Directives" folder again, looking for what I thought I had seen there in the list of hypothetical circumstances. There it was:

1, f: If any concerted attempt on the part of any person or group to remove the subject from Defense Department custody, or to aid him in any way, is made; or if the subject's existence and presence in Defense Department custody becomes public knowledge.

That sewed it up tight, and it also answered my question about Aza-Kra. Knocking out the personnel of B building would be construed as an attempt to escape or as a concerted attempt by a person or group to remove the subject from Defense Department custody, it didn't matter which. If I broke the story, it would have the same result. They would kill him.

In effect, he had put his life in my hands: and that was why he was so sure that I'd help him.

It might have been that, or what I found just before I left the office, that decided me. I don't know; I wish I did.

Coming around the desk the other way, I glanced at the thin man on the floor and noticed that there was something under him, half-hidden by his body. It turned out to be two things: a gray fedora and a pint-sized gray-leather briefcase, chained to his wrist.

So I looked under Parst's folded arms, saw the edge of a thick white sheet of paper, and pulled it out.

Under Frisbee's letterhead, it said:

By courier.

Dear General Parst:

Some possibility appears to exist that A. K. is responsible for recent disturbances in your area; please give me your thought on this as soon as possible—the decision can't be long postponed.

In the meantime you will of course consider your command under emergency status, and we count on you to use your initiative to safeguard security at all costs. In a crisis, you will consider Lieut. D. as expendable.

Sincerely yours,
CARLTON FRISBEE

cf/cf/enc.

"Enc." meant "enclosure"; I pried up Parst's arms again and found another sheet of stiff paper, folded three times, with a paperclip on it.

It was a First Lieutenant's commission, made out to Robert James Dahl, dated three days before.

If commissions can be forged, so can court-martial records.

I put the commission and the letter in my pocket. I didn't seem to feel any particular emotion, but I noticed that my hands were shaking as I sorted through the "General information" file, picked out a few sheets and stuffed them into my pocket with the other papers. I wasn't confused or in doubt about what to do next. I looked around the room, spotted a metal locker diagonally across from the filing cabinets, and opened it with one of the General's keys.

Inside were two .45 automatics, boxes of ammunition, several loaded clips, and three odd-looking sets of handcuffs, very wide and heavy, each with its key.

I took the handcuffs, the keys, both automatics and all the clips.

In a storeroom at the end of the corridor I found a two-wheeled dolly. I wheeled it all the way around to Section One and left it outside the center door. Then it struck me that I was still wearing the pinks they had given me when I arrived, and where the hell were my own clothes? I took a chance and went up to my room on the second floor, remembering that I hadn't been back there since morning.

There they were, neatly laid out on the bed. My keys, lighter, change, wallet and so on were on the bedside table. I changed and went back down to Section One.

In the gun room were two sprawled shapes, one beside the machine-gun that poked its snout through the hemispherical blister, the other under a panel set with three switches and a microphone.

The switches were clearly marked. I opened the first two, walked out and around and laid the three sets of handcuffs on the floor in the middle room. Then I went back to the gun room, closed the first two doors and opened the third.

Soft thumping sounds came from the loudspeaker over the switch panel; then the rattling of metal, more thumps, and finally a series of rattling clicks.

I opened the first door and went back inside. Through the panel in the middle door I could see Aza-Kra; he had retreated into the inner room so that all of him was plainly visible. He was squatting on the floor, his legs drawn up. His arms were at full stretch, each wrist manacled to an ankle. He strained his arms outward to show me that the cuffs were tight.

I made one more trip to open the middle door. Then I got the dolly and wheeled it in.

"Thank you," said Aza-Kra. I got a whiff of his "breath"; as Donnelly had intimated, it wasn't pleasant.

Halfway to the airport, at Aza-Kra's request, I held my

breath again. Aside from that we didn't speak except when I asked him, as I was loading him from the jeep into a limousine, "How long will they stay unconscious?"

"Not more than twenty hours, I think. I could have given them more, but I did not dare. I do not know your chemistry well enough."

We could go a long way in twenty hours. We would certainly have to.

I hated to go home, it was too obvious and there was a good chance that the hunt would start before any twenty hours were up, but there wasn't any help for it. I had a passport and a visa for England, where I had been planning to go for a publishers' conference in January, but it hadn't occurred to me to take it along on a quick trip to Washington. And now I had to have the passport.

My first idea had been to head for New York and hand Aza-Kra over to the UN there, but I saw it was no good. Extraterritoriality was just a word, like a lot of other words; we wouldn't be safe until we were out of the country, and on second thought, maybe not then.

It was a little after eight-thirty when I pulled in to the curb down the street from my house. I hadn't eaten since noon, but I wasn't hungry; and it didn't occur to me until later to think about Aza-Kra.

I got the passport and some money without waking my housekeeper. A few blocks away I parked again on a side street. I called the airport, got a reservation on the next eastbound flight, and spent half an hour buying a trunk big enough for Aza-Kra and wrestling him into it.

It struck me at the last minute that perhaps I had been counting too much on that atmosphere-plant of his. His air supply was taken care of, but what about his respiratory waste products—would he poison himself in that tiny closed space? I asked him, and he said, "No, it is all right. I will be warm, but I can bear it."

I put the lid down, then opened it again. "I forgot about food," I said. "What do you eat, anyway?"

"At Chillicothe I ate soya bean extract. With added min-

erals. But I am able to go without food for long periods.
Please, do not worry.''

All right. I put the lid down again and locked the trunk,
but I didn't stop worrying.

He was being too accommodating.

I had expected him to ask me to turn him loose, or take
him to wherever his spaceship was. He hadn't brought the
subject up; he hadn't even asked me where we were going,
or what my plans were.

I thought I knew the answer to that, but it didn't make
me any happier. He didn't ask because he already knew—
just as he'd known the contents of Parst's office, down to
the last document; just as he'd known what I was thinking
when I was in the anteroom with Donnelly.

He read minds. And he gassed people through solid metal
walls.

What else did he do?

There wasn't time to dispose of the limousine; I simply
left it at the airport. If the alarm went out before we got to
the coast, we were sunk anyhow; if not, it wouldn't matter.

Nobody stopped us. I caught the stratojet in New York at
12:20, and five hours later we were in London.

Customs was messy, but there wasn't any other way to
handle it. When we were fifth in line, I thought: *Knock them
out for about an hour*—and held my breath. Nothing happened. I rapped on the side of the trunk again to attract his
attention, and did it again. This time it worked: everybody
in sight went down like a rag doll.

I stamped my own passport, filled out a declaration form
and buried it in a stack of others, put a tag on the trunk,
loaded it aboard a handtruck, wheeled it outside and took
a cab.

I had learned something in the process, although it certainly wasn't much: either Aza-Kra couldn't, or didn't,
eavesdrop on my mind all the time—or else he was simply
one step ahead of me.

Later, on the way to the harbor, I saw a newsstand and
realized that it was going on three days since I had seen a
paper. I had tried to get the New York dailies at the airport,

but they'd been sold out—nothing on the stands but a lone copy of the Staten Island *Advance*. That hadn't struck me as odd at the time—an index of my state of mind—but it did now.

I got out and bought a copy of everything on the stand except the tipsheets—four newspapers, all of them together about equaling the bulk of one *Herald-Star*. I felt frustrated enough to ask the newsvendor if he had any papers left over from yesterday or the day before. He gave me a glassy look, made me repeat it, then pulled his face into an indescribable expression, laid a finger beside his nose, and said, " 'Arf a mo'.'' He scuttled into a bar a few yards down the street, was gone five minutes, and came back clutching a mare's-nest of soiled and bedraggled papers.

" 'Ere you are, guvnor. Three bob for the lot."

I paid him. "Thanks," I said, "very much."

He waved his hand expansively. "Okay, bud," he said. "T'ink nuttin' of it!"

A comedian.

The only Channel boat leaving before late afternoon turned out to be an excursion steamer—round trip, two guineas. The boat wasn't crowded; it was the tag-end of the season, and a rough, windy day. I found a seat without any trouble and finished sorting out my stack of papers by date and folio.

British newspapers don't customarily report any more of our news than we do of theirs, but this week our supply of catastrophes had been ample enough to make good reading across the Atlantic. I found all three of the Chicago stories—trimmed to less than two inches apiece, but there. I read the first with professional interest, the second skeptically, and the third with alarm.

I remembered the run of odd items I'd read in that Washington hotel room, a long time ago. I remembered Frisbee's letter to Parst: *"Some possibility appears to exist that A.K. is responsible for recent disturbances in your area. . . ."*

I found two of the penitentiary stories, half smothered by stop press, and I added them to the total. I drew an imaginary map of the United States in my head and stuck imaginary pins in it. Red ones, a little cluster: Des Moines, Kansas City, Decatur, St. Louis. Blue ones, a scattering around them: Chicago, Leavenworth, Terre Haute.

Down toward the end of the cabin someone's portable radio was muttering.

A fat youth in a checkered jacket had it. He moved over reluctantly and made room for me to sit down. The crisp, controlled BBC voice was saying, ". . . in Commons today, declared that Britain's trade balance is more favorable than at any time during the past fifteen years. In London, ceremonies marking the tenth anniversary of the death . . ." I let the words slide past me until I heard:

"In the United States, the mysterious epidemic affecting stockyard workers in the central states has spread to New York and New Jersey on the eastern seaboard. The President has requested Congress to provide immediate emergency meat-rationing legislation."

A blurred little woman on the bench opposite leaned forward and said, "Serve 'em right, too! Them with their beefsteak a day."

There were murmurs of approval.

I got up and went back to my own seat. . . . It all fell into one pattern, everything: the man who kicked his wife, the prize-fighters, the policeman, the wardens, the slaughterhouse "epidemic."

It was the *lex talionis*—or the Golden Rule in reverse: Be done by as you do to others.

When you injured another living thing, both of you felt the same pain. When you killed, you felt the shock of your victim's death. You might be only stunned by it, like the slaughterhouse workers, or you might die, like the policeman and the schoolboy murderer.

So-called mental anguish counted too, apparently. That explained the wave of humanitarianism in prisons, at least partially; the rest was religious hysteria and the kind of herd instinct that makes any startling new movement mushroom.

And, of course, it also explained Chillicothe: the horrible blanketing depression that settled anywhere the civilian staff congregated—the feeling of being penned up in a place where something frightful was going to happen—and the thing the two psychiatrists had been arguing about, the pseudo-claustrophobia . . . all that was nothing but the reflection of Aza-Kra's feelings, locked in that cell on an alien planet.

Be done by as you do.

And I was carrying that with me. Des Moines, Kansas City, Decatur, St. Louis, Chicago, Leavenworth, Terre Haute—*New York*. After that, England. We'd been in London less than an hour—but England is only four hundred-odd miles long, from John o' Groat's to Lands End.

I remembered what Aza-Kra had said: *Now you must learn the other law, not to kill.*

Not to kill tripeds.

My body was shaking uncontrollably; my head felt like a balloon stuffed with cotton. I stood up and looked around at the blank faces, the inward-looking eyes, every man, woman and child living in a little world of his own. I had a hysterical impulse to shout at them, *Look at you, you idiots! You've been invaded and half conquered without a shot fired, and you don't know it!*

In the next instant I realized that I was about to burst into laughter. I put my hand over my mouth and half-ran out on deck, giggles leaking through my fingers; I got to the rail and bent myself over it, roaring, apoplectic. I was utterly ashamed of myself, but I couldn't stop it; it was like a fit of vomiting.

The cold spray on my face sobered me. I leaned over the rail, looking down at the white water boiling along the hull. It occurred to me that there was one practical test still to be made: a matter of confirmation.

A middle-aged man with rheumy eyes was standing in the cabin doorway, partly blocking it. As I shouldered past him, I deliberately put my foot down on his.

An absolutely blinding pain shot through the toes of my right foot. When my eyes cleared I saw that the two of us were standing in identical attitudes—weight on one foot, the other knee bent, hand reaching instinctively for the injury.

I had taken him for a "typical Englishman," but he cursed me in a rattling stream of gutter French. I apologized, awkwardly but sincerely—very sincerely.

When we docked at Calais I still hadn't decided what to do.

What I had had in mind up till now was simply to get across France into Switzerland and hold a press conference there, inviting everybody from Tass to the UP. It had to be Switzerland for fairly obvious reasons; the English or the French would clamp a security lid on me before you could say NATO, but the Swiss wouldn't dare—they paid for their neutrality by having to look *both* ways before they cleared their throats.

I could still do that, and let the UN set up a committee to worry about Aza-Kra—but at a conservative estimate it would be ten months before the committee got its foot out of its mouth, and that would be pretty nearly ten months too late.

Or I could simply go to the American consulate in Calais and turn myself in. Within ten hours we would be back in Chillicothe, probably, and I'd be free of the responsibility. I would also be dead.

We got through customs the same way we'd done in London.

And then I had to decide.

The cab driver put his engine in gear and looked at me over his shoulder. *"Un hôtel?"*

". . . Yes," I said. "A cheap hotel. *Un hôtel à bon marché.*"

"Entendu." He jammed down the accelerator an instant before he let out the clutch; we were doing thirty before he shifted into second.

The place he took me to was a villainous third-rate commercial-travelers' hotel, smelling of urine and dirty linen. When the porters were gone I unlocked the trunk and opened it.

We stared at each other.

Moisture was beaded on his blue-gray skin, and there was a smell in the room stronger and ranker than anything that belonged there. His eyes looked duller than they had before; I could barely see the pupils.

"Well?" I said.

"You are half right," he buzzed. "I am doing it, but not for the reason you think."

"All right; you're doing it. *Stop it.* That comes first. We'll stay here, and I'll watch the papers to make sure you do."

"At the customs, those people will sleep only an hour."

"I don't give a damn. If the gendarmes come up here, you can put them to sleep. If I have to I'll move you out to the country and we'll live under a haystack. But no matter what happens we're not going a mile farther into Europe until I know you've quit. If you don't like that, you've got two choices. Either you knock me out, and see how much good it does you, or I'll take that air-machine off your head."

He buzzed inarticulately for a moment. Then, "I have to say no. It is impossible. I could stop for a time, or pretend to you that I stop, but that would solve nothing. It will be— it will do the greatest harm if I stop; you don't understand. It is necessary to continue."

I said, "That's your answer?"

"Yes. If you will let me explain—"

I stepped toward him. I didn't hold my breath, but I think half-consciously I expected him to gas me. He didn't. He didn't move; he just waited.

Seen at close range, the flesh of his head seemed to be continuous with the black substance of the cone; instead of any sharp dividing line, there was a thin area that was neither one nor the other.

I put one hand over the fleshy bulb, and felt his eyes retract and close against my palm. The sensation was indescribably unpleasant, but I kept my hand there, put the other one against the far side of the cone—pulled and pushed simultaneously, as hard as I could.

The top of my head came off.

I was leaning against the top of the open trunk, dizzy and nauseated. The pain was like a white-hot wire drawn tight around my skull just above the eyes. I couldn't see; I couldn't think.

And it didn't stop; it went on and on. . . . I pushed myself away from the trunk and let my legs fold under me. I sat on the floor with my head in my hands, pushing my fingers against the pain.

Gradually it ebbed. I heard Aza-Kra's voice buzzing very quietly, not in English but in a rhythm of tone and phrasing that seemed almost directly comprehensible; if there were a language designed to be spoken by bass viols, it might sound like that.

I got up and looked at him. Shining beads of blue liquid stood out all along the base of the cone, but the seam had not broken.

I hadn't realized that it would be so difficult, that it would be so painful. I felt the weight of the two automatics in my pockets, and I pulled one out, the metal cold and heavy in my palm . . . but I knew suddenly that I couldn't do that either.

I didn't know where his brain was, or his heart. I didn't know whether I could kill him with one shot.

I sat down on the bed, staring at him. "You knew that would happen, didn't you," I said. "You must think I'm a prize sucker."

He said nothing. His eyes were half-closed, and a thin whey-colored fluid was drooling out of the two mouths I could see. Aza-Kra was being sick.

I felt an answering surge of nausea. Then the flow stopped, and a second later, the nausea stopped too. I felt angry, and frustrated, and frightened.

After a moment I got up off the bed and started for the door.

"Please," said Aza-Kra. "Will you be gone long?"

"I don't know," I said. "Does it matter?"

"If you will be gone long," he said, "I would ask that you loosen the handcuffs for a short period before you go."

I stared at him, suddenly hating him with a violence that shook me.

"No," I said, and reached for the door-handle.

My body knotted itself together like a fist. My legs gave way under me, and I missed the door-handle going down; I hit the floor hard.

There was no sensation in my hands or feet. The muscles

of my shoulders, arms, thighs, and calves were one huge, heavy pain. And I couldn't move.

I looked at Aza-Kra's wrists, shackled to his drawn-up ankles. He had been like that for something like fourteen hours.

"I am sorry," said Aza-Kra. "I did not want to do that to you, but there was no other way."

I thought dazedly, *No other way to do what?*

"To make you wait. To listen. To let me explain."

I said, "I don't get it." Anger flared again, then faded under something more intense and painful. The closest English word for it is "humility"; some other language may come nearer, but I doubt it; it isn't an emotion that we like to talk about. I felt bewildered, and ashamed, and very small, all at once, and there was another component, harder to name. A . . . threshold feeling.

I tried again. "I felt the other pain, before, but not this. Is that because—"

"Yes. There must be the intention to injure or cause pain. I will tell you why. I have to go back very far. When an animal becomes more developed—many cells, instead of one—always the same things happen. I am the first man of my kind who ever saw a man of your kind. But we both have eyes. We both have ears." The feathery spines on his neck stiffened and relaxed. "Also there is another sense that always comes. But always it goes only a little way and then stops.

"When you are a young animal, fighting with the others to live, it is useful to have a sense which feels the thoughts of the enemy. Just as it is useful to have a sense which sees the shape of his body. But this sense cannot come all at once, it must grow by a little and a little, as when a surface that can tell the light from the dark becomes a true eye.

"But the easiest thoughts to feel are pain thoughts, they are much stronger than any others. And when the sense is still weak—it is a part of the brain, not an organ by itself—when it is weak, only the strongest stimulus can make it work. This stimulus is hatred, or anger, or the wish to kill.

"So that just when the sense is enough developed that it

could begin to be useful, it always disappears. It is not gone, it is pushed under. A very long time ago, one race discovered this sense and learned how it could be brought back. It is done by a class of organic chemicals. You have not the word. For each race a different member of the class, but always it can be done. The chemical is a catalyst, it is not used up. The change it makes is in the cells of all the body—it is permanent, it passes also to the children.

"You understand, when a race is older, to kill is not useful. With the change, true civilization begins. The first race to find this knowledge gave it to others, and those to others, and now all have it. All who are able to leave their planets. We give it to you, now, because you are ready. When you are older there will be others who are ready. You will give it to them."

While I had been listening, the pain in my arms and legs had slowly been getting harder and harder to take. I reminded myself that Aza-Kra had borne it, probably, at least ten hours longer than I had; but that didn't make it much easier. I tried to keep my mind off it but that wasn't possible; the band of pain around my head was still there, too, a faint throbbing. And both were consequences of things I had done to Aza-Kra. I was suffering with him, measure for measure.

Justice. Surely that was a good thing? Automatic instant retribution, mathematically accurate: an eye for an eye.

I said, "That was what you were doing when they caught you, then—finding out which chemical we reacted to?"

"Yes. I did not finish until after they had brought me to Chillicothe. Then it was much more difficult. If not for my accident, all would have gone much more quickly."

"The walls?"

"Yes. As you have guessed, my air machine will also make other substances and expel them with great force. Also, when necessary, it will place these substances in a— state of matter, you have not the word—so that they pass through solid objects. But this takes much power. While in Chillicothe my range was very small. Later, when I can be in the open, it will be much greater."

He caught what I was thinking before I had time to speak. He said, "Yes. You will agree. When you understand."

It was the same thing he had told me at Chillicothe, almost to the word.

I said, "You keep talking about this thing as a gift but I notice you didn't ask us if we wanted it. What kind of a gift is that?"

"You are not serious. You know what happened when I was captured."

After a moment he added, "I think if it had been possible, if we could have asked each man and woman on the planet to say yes or no, explaining everything, showing that there was no trick, that most would have said yes. For people the change is good. But for governments it is not good."

I said, "I'd like to believe you. It would be very pleasant to believe you. But nothing you can say changes the fact that this thing, this gift of yours could be a weapon. To soften us up before you move in. If you were an advance agent for an invasion fleet, this is what you'd be doing."

"You are thinking with habits," he said. "Try to think with logic. Imagine that your race is very old, with much knowledge. You have ships that cross between the stars. Now you discover this young race, these Earthmen, who only begin to learn to leave their own planet. You decide to conquer them. Why? What is your reason?"

"How do I know? It could be anything. It might be something I couldn't even imagine. For all I know you want to eat us."

His throat-spines quivered. He said slowly, "You are partly serious. You really think . . . I am sorry that you did not read the studies of the physiologists. If you had, you would know. My digestion is only for vegetable food. You cannot understand, but—with us, to eat meat is like with you, to eat excretions."

I said, "All right, maybe we have something else you want. Natural resources that you've used up. Some substance, maybe some rare element."

"This is still habit thinking. Have you forgotten my air machine?"

"—Or maybe you just want the planet itself. With us cleared off it, to make room for you."

"Have you never looked at the sky at night?"

I said, "All *right*. But this quiz was your idea, not mine. I *admit* that I don't know enough even to make a sensible guess at your motives. And that's the reason why I can't trust you."

He was silent a moment. Then: "Remember that the substance which makes the change is a catalyst. Also it is a very fine powder. The particles are of only a few molecules each. The winds carry it. It is swallowed and breathed in and absorbed by the skin. It is breathed out and excreted. The wind takes it again. Water carries it. It is carried by insects and by birds and animals, and by men, in their bodies and in their clothing.

"This you can understand and know that it is true. If I die another could come and finish what I have begun, but even this is not necessary. The amount of the catalyst I have already released is more than enough. It will travel slowly, but nothing can stop it. If I die now, this instant, still in a year the catalyst will reach every part of the planet."

After a long time I said, "Then what did you mean by saying that a great harm would be done, if you stopped now?"

"I meant this. Until now, only your Western nations have the catalyst. In a few days their time of crisis will come, beginning with the United States. And the nations of the East will attack."

IV

I FOUND THAT I COULD MOVE, INCHMEAL, IF I SWEATED hard enough at it. It took me what seemed like half an hour to get my hand into my pocket, paw all the stuff out onto the floor, and get the keyring hooked over one finger. Then I had to crawl about ten feet to Aza-Kra, and when I got there my fingers simply couldn't hold the keys firmly enough.

I picked them up in my teeth and got two of the wrist-cuffs unlocked. That was the best I could do; the other one was behind him, inside the trunk, and neither of us had strength enough to pull him out where I could get at it.

It was comical. My muscles weren't cramped, but my nervous system was getting messages that said they were—so, to all intents and purposes, it was true. I had no control over it; the human body is about as skeptical as a God-smitten man at a revival meeting. If mine had thought it was burning, I would have developed simon-pure blisters.

Then the pins-and-needles started, as Aza-Kra began to flex his arms and legs to get the stiffness out of them. Between us, after a while, we got him out of the trunk and unlocked the third cuff. In a few minutes I had enough

freedom of movement to begin massaging his cramped
muscles; but it was three-quarters of an hour before either
of us could stand.

We caught the mid-afternoon plane to Paris, with Aza-
Kra in the trunk again. I checked into a hotel, left him
there, and went shopping: I bought a hideous black dress
with imitation-onyx trimming, a black coat with a cape, a
feather muff, a tall black hat and the heaviest mourning veil
I could find. At a theatrical costumer's near the Place de
l'Opera I got a reasonably lifelike old-woman mask and a
heavy wig.

When he was dressed up, the effect was startling. The
tall hat covered the cone, the muff covered two of his hands.
There was nothing to be done about the feet, but the skirt
hung almost to the ground, and I thought he would pass
with luck.

We got a cab and headed for the American consulate, but
halfway there I remembered about the photographs. We
stopped off at an amusement arcade and I got my picture
taken in a coin-operated machine. Aza-Kra was another
problem—that mask wouldn't fool anybody without the
veil—but I spotted a poorly-dressed old woman and with
some difficulty managed to make her understand that I was
a crazy American who would pay her fifty francs to pose
for her picture. We struck a bargain at a hundred.

As soon as we got into the consulate waiting-room, Aza-
Kra gassed everybody in the building. I locked the street
door and searched the offices until I found a man with a
little pile of blank passport books on the desk in front of
him. He had been filling one in on a machine like a type-
writer except that it had a movable plane-surface platen instead of a cylinder.

I moved him out of the way and made out two passports;
one for myself, as Arthur James LeRoux; one for Aza-Kra,
as Mrs. Adrienne LeRoux. I pasted on the photographs and
fed them into the machine that pressed the words "Photograph attached U. S. Consulate Paris, France" into the
paper, and then into the one that impressed the consular
seal.

I signed them, and filled in the blanks on the inside covers, in the taxi on the way to the Israeli consulate. The afternoon was running out, and we had a lot to do.

We went to six foreign consulates, gassed the occupants, and got a visa stamp in each one. I had the devil's own time filling them out; I had to copy the scribbles I found in legitimate passports at each place and hope for the best. The Israeli one was surprisingly simple, but the Japanese was a horror.

We had dinner in our hotel room—steak for me, water and soy-bean paste, bought at a health-food store, for Aza-Kra. Just before we left for Le Bourget, I sent a cable to Eli Freeman:

> BIG STORY WILL HAVE TO WAIT SPREAD THIS NOW ALL STOCKYARD SO-CALLED EPIDEMIC AND SIMILAR PHE-NOMENA DUE ONE CAUSE STEP ON SOMEBODY'S TOE TO SEE WHAT I MEAN.

Shortly after seven o'clock we were aboard a flight bound for the Middle East.

And that was the fourth day, during which a number of things happened that I didn't have time to add to my list until later.

Commercial and amateur fisherman along the Atlantic seaboard, from Delaware Bay as far north as Portland, suffered violent attacks whose symptoms resembled those of asthma. Some, who had been using rods or poles rather than nets, complained also of sharp pains in the jaws and hard palate. Three deaths were reported.

The "epidemic" now covered roughly half the continental United States. All livestock shipments from the West had been canceled, stockyards in the affected area were full to bursting. The President had declared a national emergency.

Lobster had disappeared completely from East Coast menus.

One Robert James Dahl, described as the owner and publisher of a Middle Western newspaper, was being sought by the Defense Department and the FBI in connection with the disappearance of certain classified documents.

The next day, the fifth, was Saturday. At two in the morning on a Sabbath, Tel Aviv seemed as dead as Angkor. We had four hours there, between planes; we could have spent them in the airport waiting room, but I was wakeful and wanted to talk to Aza-Kra. There was one ancient taxi at the airport; I had the driver take us into the town and leave us there, down in the harbor section, until plane time.

We sat on a bench behind the sea wall and watched the moonlight on the Mediterranean. Parallel banks of faintly-silvered clouds arched over us to northward; the air was fresh and cool.

After a while I said, "You know that I'm only playing this your way for one reason. As far as the rest of it goes, the more I think about it the less I like it."

"Why?"

"A dozen reasons. The biological angle, for one. I don't like violence, I don't like war, but it doesn't matter what I like. They're biologically necessary, they eliminate the unfit."

"Do you say that only the unfit are killed in wars?"

"That isn't what I mean. In modern war the contest isn't between individuals, it's between whole populations. Nations, and groups of nations. It's a cruel, senseless, wasteful business, and when you're in the middle of it it's hard to see any good at all in it, but it works—the survivors *survive*, and that's the only test there is."

"Our biologists do not take this view." He added, "Neither do yours."

I said, "How's that?"

"Your biologists agree with ours that war is not biological. It is social. When so many are killed, no stock improves. All suffer. It is as you yourself say, the contest is between nations. But their wars kill men."

I said, "All right, I concede that one. But we're not the only kind of animal on this planet, and we didn't get to be the dominant species without fighting. What are we supposed to do if we run into a hungry lion—argue with him?"

"In a few weeks there will be no more lions."

I stared at him. "This affects lions, too? Tigers, elephants, everything?"

"Everything of sufficient brain. Roughly, everything above the level of your insects."

"But I understood you to say that the catalyst—that it took a different catalyst for each species."

"No. All those with spines and warm blood have the same ancestors. Your snakes may perhaps need a different catalyst, and I believe you have some primitive sea creatures which kill, but they are not important."

I said, "My God." I thought of lions, wolves, coyotes, housecats, lying dead beside their prey. Eagles, hawks and owls tumbling out of the sky. Ferrets, stoats, weasels . . .

The world a big garden, for protected children.

My fists clenched. "But this is a million times worse than I had any idea. It's insane. You're upsetting the whole natural balance, you're knocking it crossways. Just for a start, what the hell are we going to do about rats and mice? That's—" I choked on my tongue. There were too many images in my mind to put any of them into words. Rats like a tidal wave, filling a street from wall to wall. Deer swarming out of the forests. The sky blackening with crows, sparrows, jays.

"It will be difficult for some years," Aza-Kra said. "Perhaps even as difficult as you now think. But you say that to fight for survival is good. Is it not better to fight against other species than among yourselves?"

"Fight!" I said. "What have you left us to fight with? How many rats can a man kill before he drops dead from shock?"

"It is possible to kill without causing pain or shock. . . . You would have thought of this, although it is a new idea for you. Even your killing of animals for food can continue. We do not ask you to become as old as we are in a day. Only to put behind you your cruelty which has no purpose."

He had answered me, as always; and as always, the answer was two-edged. It was possible to kill painlessly, yes. And the only weapon Aza-Kra had brought to Earth, apparently, was an anesthetic gas. . . .

We landed at Srinagar, in the Vale of Kashmir, at high
noon: a sea of white light under a molten-metal sky.

Crossing the field, I saw a group of white-turbaned figures standing at the gate. I squinted at them through the
glare; heat-waves made them jump and waver, but in a moment I was sure. They were bush-bearded Sikh policemen,
and there were eight of them.

I pressed Aza-Kra's arm sharply and held my breath.

A moment later we picked our way through the sprawled
line of passengers to the huddle of bodies at the gate. The
passport examiner, a slender Hindu, lay a yard from the
Sikhs. I plucked a sheet of paper out of his hand.

Sure enough, it was a list of the serial numbers of the passports we had stolen from the Paris consulate.

Bad luck. It was only six-thirty in Paris now, and on a
Saturday morning at that; we should have had at least six
hours more. But something could have gone wrong at any
of the seven consulates—an after-hours appointment, or a
worried wife, say. After that the whole thing would have
unraveled.

"How much did you give them this time?" I asked.

"As before. Twenty hours."

"All right, good. Let's go."

He had overshot his range a little: all four of the hack-
drivers waiting outside the airport building were snoring
over their wheels. I dumped the skinniest one in the back
seat with Aza-Kra and took over.

Not for the first time, it occurred to me that without me
or somebody just like me Aza-Kra would be helpless. It
wasn't just a matter of getting out of Chillicothe; he couldn't
drive a car or fly a plane, he couldn't pass for human by
himself; he couldn't speak without giving himself away.
Free, with no broken bones, he could probably escape re-
capture indefinitely; but if he wanted to go anywhere he
would have to walk.

And not for the first time, I tried to see into a history
book that hadn't been written yet. My name was there, that
much was certain, providing there was going to be any history to write. But was it a name like Blondel . . . or did it
sound more like Vidkun Quisling?

We had to go south; there was nothing in any other direction but the highest mountains in the world. We didn't have Pakistan visas, so Lahore and Amritsar, the obvious first choices, were out. The best we could do was Chamba, about two hundred rail miles southeast on the Srinagar-New Delhi line. It wasn't on the principal air routes, but we could get a plane there to Saharanpur, which was.

There was an express leaving in half an hour, and we took it. I bought an English-language newspaper at the station and read it backward and forward for four hours; Aza-Kra spent the time apparently asleep, with his cone, hidden by the black hat, tilted out the window.

The "epidemic" had spread to five Western states, plus Quebec, Ontario and Manitoba, and parts of Mexico and Cuba . . . plus England and France, I knew, but there was nothing about that in my Indian paper; too early.

In Chamba I bought the most powerful battery-operated portable radio I could find; I wished I had thought of it sooner. I checked with the airport: there was a flight leaving Saharanpur for Port Blair at eight o'clock.

Port Blair, in the Andamans, is Indian territory; we wouldn't need to show our passports. What we were going to do after that was another question.

I could have raided another set of consulates, but I knew it would be asking for trouble. Once was bad enough; twice, and when we tried it a third time—as we would have to, unless I found some other answer—I was willing to bet we would find them laying for us, with gas masks and riot guns.

Somehow, in the few hours we were to spend at Port Blair, I had to get those serial numbers altered by an expert.

We had been walking the black, narrow dockside streets for two hours when Aza-Kra suddenly stopped.

"Something?"

"Wait," he said. ". . . Yes. This is the man you are looking for. He is a professional forger. His name is George Wheelwright. He can do it, but I do not know whether he will. He is a very timid and suspicious man."

"All right. In here?"

"Yes."

We went up a narrow unlighted stairway, choked with a kitchen-midden of smells, curry predominating. At the second-floor landing Aza-Kra pointed to a door. I knocked.

Scufflings behind the door. A low voice: "Who's that?"

"A friend. Let us in, Wheelwright."

The door cracked open and yellow light spilled out; I saw the outline of a head and the faint gleam of a bulbous eye. "What d'yer want?"

"Want you to do a job for me, Wheelwright. Don't keep us talking here in the hall."

The door opened wider and I squeezed through into a cramped, untidy box of a kitchen. A faded cloth covered the doorway to the next room.

Wheelwright glanced at Aza-Kra and then stared hard at me; he was a little chicken-breasted wisp of a man, dressed in dungarees and a striped polo shirt. "Who sent yer?"

"You wouldn't know the name. A friend of mine in Calcutta." I took out the passports. "Can you fix these?"

He looked at them carefully, taking his time. "What's wrong with 'em?"

"Nothing but the serial numbers."

"What's wrong with *them*?"

"They're on a list."

He laughed, a short, meaningless bark.

I said, "Well?"

"Who'd yer say yer friend in Calcutter was?"

"I haven't any friend in Calcutta. Never mind how I knew about you. Will you do the job or won't you?"

He handed the passports back and moved toward the door. "Mister, I haven't got the time to fool with yer. Perhaps yer having me on, or perhaps yer've made an honest mistake. There's another Wheelwright over on the north side of town. You try him." He opened the door. "Good night, both."

I pushed it shut again and reached for him, but he was a yard away in one jump, like a rabbit. He stood beside the table, arms hanging, and stared at me with a vague smile.

I said, "I haven't got time to play games, either. I'll pay

you five hundred American dollars to alter these pass-ports—'' I tossed them onto the table—"or else I'll beat the living tar out of you.'' I took a step toward him.

I never saw a man move faster: he had the drawer open and the gun out and aimed before I finished that step. But the muzzle trembled slightly. "No nearer,'' he said hoarsely.

I thought, *Five minutes*, and held my breath.

When he slumped, I picked up the revolver. Then I lifted him—he weighed about ninety pounds—propped him in a chair behind the table, and waited.

In a few minutes he raised his head and goggled at me dazedly. "How'd yer do that?'' he whispered.

I put the money on the table beside the passports. "Start,'' I said.

He stared at it, then at me. His thin lips tightened. "Go ter blazes,'' he said.

I stepped around the table and cuffed him backhand. I felt the blow on my own face, hard and stinging, but I did it again. I kept it up. It wasn't pleasant; I was feeling not only the blows themselves, but Wheelwright's emotional re-sponses, the shame and wretchedness and anger, and the queasy writhing fear: Wheelwright couldn't bear pain.

At that, he beat me. When I stopped, sickened and dizzy, and said as roughly as I could. "Had enough, Wheel-wright?'' he answered, "Not if yer was ter kill me, yer bloody barstid.''

His voice trembled, and his face was streaked with tears, but he meant it. He thought I was a government agent, try-ing to bully him into signing his own prison sentence, and rather than let me do it he would take any amount of pun-ishment; prison was the one thing he feared more than phys-ical pain.

I looked at Aza-Kra. His neck-spines were erect and quivering; I could see the tips of them at the edges of the veil. Then inspiration hit me.

I pulled him forward where the little man could see him, and lifted the veil. The feathery spines stood out clearly on either side of the corpse-white mask.

"I won't touch you again," he said. "But look at this. Can you see?"

His eyes widened; he scrubbed them with the palms of his hands and looked again.

"And this," I said. I pulled at Aza-Kra's forearm and the clawed blue-gray hand came out of the muff.

Wheelwright's eyes bulged. He flattened himself against the back of the chair.

"Now," I said, "six hundred dollars—or I'll take this mask off and show you what's behind it."

He clenched his eyes shut. His face had gone yellowish-pale; his nostrils were white.

"Get it out of here," he said faintly.

He didn't move until Aza-Kra had disappeared behind the curtain into the other room. Then, without a word, he poured and drank half a tumblerful of whisky, switched on a gooseneck lamp, produced bottles, pens and brushes from the table drawer, and went to work. He bleached away the first and last digits of both serial numbers, then painted over the areas with a thin wash of color that matched the blue tint of the paper. With a jeweler's loupe in his eye, he restored the obliterated tiny letters of the background design; finally, still using the loupe, he drew the new digits in black. From first to last, it took him thirty minutes; and his hands didn't begin to tremble until he was done.

V

THE SIXTH DAY WAS TWO DAYS—BECAUSE WE LEFT OTARU at 3:30 p.m. Sunday and arrived at Honolulu at 4:00 a.m. Saturday. We had lost five hours in traversing sixty-one degrees of longitude—but we'd also gained a day by crossing the International Date Line from west to east.

On the sixth day, then, which was two days, the following things happened and were duly reported:

Be Done By As Ye Do was the title of some thousands of sermons and, by count, more than seven hundred front-page newspaper editorials from Newfoundland to Oaxaca. My cable to Freeman had come a little late; the *Herald Star's* announcement was lost in the ruck.

Following this, a wave of millennial enthusiasm swept the continent; Christians and Jews everywhere feasted, fasted, prayed and in other ways celebrated the imminent Second (or First) Coming of Christ. Evangelistic and fundamentalist sects garnered souls by the million.

Members of the Apostolic Overcoming Holy Church of God, the Pentecostal Fire Baptized Holiness Church and numerous other groups gave away most or all of their worldly possessions. Others were more practical. The Seventh Day Adventists, who are vegetarians, pooled capital and began an enormous expansion of their meatless-food factories, dairies and other enterprises.

Delegates to a World Synod of Christian Churches began arriving at a tent city near Smith Center, Kansas, late Saturday night. Trouble developed almost immediately between the Brethren Church of God (Reformed Dunkers) and the Two-Seed-in-the-Spirit Predestinarian Baptists, later spreading to a schism which led to the establishment of two rump synods, one at Lebanon and the other at Athol.

Five hundred Doukhobors stripped themselves mother-naked, burned their homes, and marched on Vancouver.

Roman Catholics in most places celebrated the Feast of the Transfiguration as usual, awaiting advice from Rome.

Riots broke out in Chicago, Detroit, New Orleans, Philadelphia and New York. In each case the original disturbances were brief, but were followed by protracted vandalism and looting which local police, state police, and even National Guard units were unable to check. By midnight Sunday property damage was estimated at more than twenty million dollars. The casualty list was fantastically high. So was the proportion of police-and-National-Guard casualties—exactly fifty percent of the total.

In the British Isles, Western Europe and Scandinavia, the early symptoms of the Western hemisphere's disaster were beginning to appear: the stricken slaughterers and fishermen, the unease in prisons, the freaks of violence.

An unprecedented number of political refugees turned up on the West German side of the Burnt Corridor early Saturday morning.

Late the same day, a clash between Sikh and Moslem guards on the India–Pakistan border near Sialkot resulted in the annihilation of both parties.

And on Sunday it hit the fighting in Indo-China.

Allied and Communist units, engaging at sixty points along the eight-hundred-mile front, fell back with the heaviest casualties of the war.

Red bombers launched a successful daylight attack on Luangprabang: successful, that is, except that nineteen out of twenty planes crashed outside the city or fell into the Nam Ou.

Forty Allied bombers took off on sorties to Yen-bay, Hanoi and Nam-dinh. None returned.

Nobody knew it yet, but the war was over.

Still other things happened but were not recorded by the press:

A man in Arizona, a horse gelder by profession, gave up his business and moved out of the county, alleging ill health.

So did a dentist in Tacoma, and another in Galveston.

In Breslau an official of the People's Police resigned his position with the same excuse; and one in Buda; and one in Pest.

A conservative Tajik tribesman of Indarab, discovering that his new wife had been unfaithful, attempted to deal with her in the traditional manner, but desisted when a critical observer would have said he had hardly begun; nor did this act of compassion bring him any relief.

And outside the town of Otaru, just two hundred and fifty miles from the Sea of Japan from the eastern shore of the Russian Socialist Federated Soviet Republic, Aza-Kra used his anesthetic gas again—on me.

I had been bone-tired when we left Port Blair shortly before midnight, but I hadn't slept all the long dark droning way to Manila; or from there to Tokyo, with the sun rising half an hour after we cleared the Philippines and slowly turning the globe underneath us to a white disk of fire; or from Tokyo north again to Otaru, bleak and windy and smelling of brine.

In all that time, I hadn't been able to forget Wheelwright except for half an hour toward the end, when I picked up an English-language broadcast from Tokyo and heard the news from the States.

The first time you burn yourself playing with matches, the chances are that if the blisters aren't too bad, you get over it fast enough; you forget about it. But the second time, it's likely to sink in.

Wheelwright was my second time; Wheelwright finished me.

It's more than painful, it's more than frightening, to cause another living creature pain and feel what he feels. It tears you apart. It makes you the victor and the victim, and neither half of that is bearable.

It makes you love what you destroy—as you love yourself—and makes you hate yourself as your victim hates you.

That isn't all. I had felt Wheelwright's self-loathing as his body cringed and the tears spilled out of his eyes, the helpless gut-twisting shame that was as bad as the fear; and that burden was on me too.

Wheelwright was talented. That was his own achievement; he had found it in himself and developed it and trained himself to use it. Wheelwright had courage. That was his own. But who had made Wheelwright afraid? And who had taught him that the world was his enemy?

You, and I, and every other human being on the planet, and all our two-legged ancestors before us. Because we had settled for too little. Because not more than a handful of us, out of all the crawling billions, had ever had the will to break the chain of blows, from father to daughter to son, generation after generation.

So there was Wheelwright; that was what we had made out of him: the artistry and the courage compressed to a needle-thin, needle-hard core inside him, and that only because we hadn't been able to destroy it altogether; the rest of him self-hatred, and suspicion, and resentment, and fear.

But after breakfast in Tokyo, it began to seem a little more likely that some kind of a case could be made for the continued existence of the human race. And after that it was natural to think about lions, and about the rioting that was going on in America.

For all his moral nicety, Aza-Kra had no trouble in justifying the painful extinction of carnivores. From his point of view, they were better off dead. It was regrettable, of course, but . . .

But, *sub specie aeternitatis*, was a man much different from a lion?

It was a commonplace that no other animal killed on so

grand a scale as man. The problem had never come up before: could we live without killing?

I was standing with Aza-Kra at the top of a little hill that overlooked the coast road and the bay. The bus that had brought us there was dwindling, a white speck in a cloud of dust, down the highway toward Cape Kamui.

Aza-Kra sat on a stone, his third leg grotesquely bulging the skirt of his coat. His head was bent forward, as if the old woman he was pretending to be had fallen asleep, chin on massive chest; the conical hat pointed out to sea.

I said, "This is the time of crisis you were talking about, for America."

"Yes. It begins now."

"When does it end? Let's talk about this a little more. This justice. Crimes of violence—all right. They punish themselves, and before long they'll prevent themselves automatically. What about crimes of property? A man steals my wallet and runs. Or he smashes a window and takes what he wants. Who's going to stop him?"

He didn't answer for a moment; when he did the words came slowly and the pronunciation was bad, as if he were too weary to attend to it. "The wallet can be chained to your clothing. The window can be made of glass that does not break."

I said impatiently, "You know that's not what I mean. I'm talking about the problem as it affects everybody. We solve it by policemen and courts and prisons. What do we do instead?"

"I am sorry that I did not understand you. Give me a moment. . . ."

I waited.

"In your Middle Ages, when a man was insane, what did you do?"

I thought of Bedlam, and of creatures with matted hair chained to rooftops.

He didn't wait for me to speak. "Yes. And now, you are more wise?"

"A little."

"Yes. And in the beginning of your Industrial Revolution, when a factory stopped and men had no work, what was done?''

"They starved."

"And now?"

"There are relief organizations. We try to keep them alive until they can get work.''

"If a man steals what he does not need," Aza-Kra said, "is he not sick? If a man steals what he must have to live, can you blame him?''

Socrates, in an onyx-trimmed dress, three-legged on a stone.

Finally I said, "It's easy enough to make us look foolish, but we have made some progress in the last two thousand years. Now you want us to go the rest of the way overnight. It's impossible; we haven't got time enough.''

"You will have more time now." His voice was very faint. "Killing wastes much time. . . . Forgive me, now I must sleep.''

His head dropped even farther forward. I watched for a while to see if he would topple over, but of course he was too solidly based. A tripod. I sat down beside him, feeling my own fatigue drag at my body, envying him his rest; but I couldn't sleep.

There was really no point in arguing with him, I told myself; he was too good for me. I was a savage splitting logic with a missionary. He knew more than I did; probably he was more intelligent. And the central question, the only one that mattered, couldn't be answered the way I was going at it.

Aza-Kra himself was the key, not the doctrine of non-violence, not the psychology of crime.

If he was telling the truth about himself and the civilization he came from, I had nothing to worry about.

If he wasn't, then I should have left him in Chillicothe or killed him in Paris; and if I could kill him now, that was what I should do.

And I didn't know. After all this time, I still didn't know.

I saw the bus come back down the road and disappear toward Otaru. After a long time, I saw it heading out again. When it came back from the cape the second time, I woke

Aza-Kra and we slogged down the steep path to the roadside. I waved as the bus came nearer; it slowed and rattled to a halt a few yards beyond us.

Passengers' heads popped out of the windows to watch us as we walked toward the door. Most of them were Japanese, but I saw one Caucasian, leaning with both arms out of the window. I saw his features clearly, narrow pale nose and lips, blue eyes behind rimless glasses; sunlight glinting on sparse yellow hair. And then I saw the flat dusty road coming up to meet me.

I was lying face-up on a hard sandy slope; when I opened my eyes I saw the sky and a few blades of tough, dry grass. The first thought that came into my head was *Now I know. Now I've had it.*

I sat up. And a buzzing voice said, "Hold your breath!"

Turning, I saw a body sprawled on the slope just below me. It was the yellow-haired man. Beyond him squatted the gray form of Aza-Kra.

"All right," he said.

I let my breath out. "What—?"

He showed me a brown metal ovoid, cross-hatched with fragmentation grooves. A grenade.

"He was about to arm it. There was no time to warn you. I knew you would wish to see for yourself."

I looked around dazedly. Thirty feet above, the slope ended in a clean-cut line against the sky; beyond it was a short, narrow white strip that I recognized as the top of the bus, still parked at the side of the road.

"We have ten minutes more before the others awaken."

I went through the man's pockets. I found a handful of change, a wallet with nothing in it but a few yen notes, and a folded slip of glossy white paper. That was all.

I unfolded the paper, but I knew what it was even before I saw the small teleprinted photograph on its inner side. It was a copy of my passport picture—the one on the genuine document, not the bogus one I had made in Paris.

On the way back, my hands began shaking. It got so bad that I had to put them between my thighs and squeeze hard;

and then the shaking spread to my legs and arms and jaw. My forehead was cold and there was a football-sized ache in my belly, expanding to a white pain every time we hit a bump. The whole bus seemed to be tilting ponderously over to the right, farther and farther but never falling down.

Later, when I had had a cup of coffee and two cigarettes in the terminal lunchroom, I got one of the most powerful irrational impulses I've ever known: I wanted to take the next bus back to that spot on the coast road, walk down the slope to where the yellow-haired man was, and kick his skull to flinders.

If we were lucky, the yellow-haired man might have been the only one in Otaru who knew we were here. The only way to find out was to go on to the airport and take a chance; either way, we had to get out of Japan. But it didn't end there. Even if they didn't know where we were now, they knew all the stops on our itinerary; they knew which visas we had. Maybe Aza-Kra would be able to gas the next one before he killed us, and then again maybe not.

I thought about Frisbee and Parst and the President—damning them all impartially—and my anger grew. By now, I realized suddenly, they must have understood that we were responsible for what was happening. They would have been energetically apportioning the blame for the last few days; probably Parst had already been court-martialed.

Once that was settled, there would be two things they could do next. They could publish the truth, admit their own responsibility, and warn the world. Or they could destroy all the evidence and keep silent. If the world went to hell in a bucket, at least they wouldn't be blamed for it. . . . Providing I was dead. Not much choice.

After another minute I got up and Aza-Kra followed me out to a taxi. We stopped at the nearest telegraph office and I sent a wire to Frisbee in Washington:

HAVE SENT FULL ACCOUNT CHILLICOTHE TO TRUST-
WORTHY PERSON WITH INSTRUCTIONS PUBLISH EVENT
MY DEATH OR DISAPPEARANCE. CALL OFF YOUR DOGS.

It was childish, but apparently it worked. Not only did we have no trouble at Otaru airport—the yellow-haired man, as I'd hoped, must have been working alone—but nobody bothered us at Honolulu or Asuncion.

Just the same, the mood of depression and nervousness that settled on me that day didn't lift; it grew steadily worse. Fourteen hours' sleep in Asuncion didn't mend it; Monday's reports of panics and bank failures in North America intensified it, but that was incidental.

And when I slept, I had nightmares: dreams of stifling-dark jungles, full of things with teeth.

We spent twenty-four hours in Asuncion, while Aza-Kra pumped out enough catalyst to blanket South America's seven million square miles—a territory almost as big as the sprawling monster of Soviet Eurasia.

After that we flew to Capetown—and that was it. We were finished.

We had spiraled around the globe, from the United States to England, to France, to Israel, to India, to Japan, to Paraguay, to the Union of South Africa, trailing an expanding invisible cloud behind us. Now the winds were carrying it westward from the Atlantic, south from the Mediterranean, north from the Indian Ocean, west from the Pacific.

Frigate birds and locusts, men in tramp steamers and men in jet planes would carry it farther. In a week it would have reached all the places we had missed: Australia, Micronesia, the islands of the South Pacific, the Poles.

That left the lunar bases and the orbital stations, Ours and Theirs. But they had to be supplied from Earth; the infection would come to them in rockets.

For better or worse, we had what we had always said we wanted. Ahimsa. The Age of Reason. The Kingdom of God.

And I still didn't know whether I was Judas, or the little Dutch boy with his finger in the dike.

I didn't find out until three weeks later.

We stayed on in Capetown, resting and waiting. Listening to the radio and reading newspapers kept me occupied a good part of the time. When restlessness drove me out of doors, I wandered aimlessly in the business section, or went down to the harbor and spent hours staring out past the castle and the breakwater.

But my chief occupation, the thing that obsessed me now, was the study of Aza-Kra.

He seemed very tired. His skin was turning dry and rough, more gray than blue; his eyes were blue-threaded and more opaque-looking than ever. He slept a great deal and moved little. The soybean paste I was able to get for him gave him insufficient nourishment; vitamins and minerals were lacking.

I asked him why he didn't make what he needed in his air machine. He said that some few of the compounds could be inhaled, and he was making those; that he had had another transmuter, for food-manufacture, but that it had been taken from him; and that he would be all right; he would last until his friends came.

He didn't know when that would be; or he wouldn't tell me.

His speech was slower and his diction more slurred each day. It was obviously difficult for him to talk; but I goaded him, I nagged him, I would not let him alone. I spent days on one topic, left it, came back to it and asked the same questions over. I made copious notes of what he said and the way he said it.

I wanted to learn to read the signs of his emotions; or failing that, to catch him in a lie.

A dozen times I thought I had trapped him into a contradiction, and each time, wearily, patiently, he explained what I had misunderstood. As for his emotions, they had only one visible sign that I was able to discover; the stiffening and trembling of his neck-spines.

Gestures of emotion are arbitrary. There are human tribes whose members never smile. There are others who smile when they are angry. Cf. Dodgson's Cheshire Cat.

He was doing it more and more often as the time went by; but what did it mean? Anger? Resentment? Annoyance? *Amusement?*

The riots in the United States ended on the 9th and 10th when interfaith committees toured each city in loud-speaker trucks. Others began elsewhere.

Business was at a standstill in most larger cities. Galveston, Nashville and Birmingham joined in celebrating Hallelujah Week: dancing in the streets, bonfires day and night, every church and every bar roaring wide open.

Russia's delegate to the United Nations, who had been larding his speeches with mock-sympathetic references to the Western nations' difficulties, arose on the 9th and delivered a furious three-hour tirade accusing the entire non-Communist world of cowardly cryptofascistic biological warfare against the Soviet Union and the People's Republics of Europe and Asia.

The new staffs of the Federal penitentiaries in America, in office less than a week, followed their predecessors in mass resignations. The last official act of the wardens of Leavenworth, Terre Haute and Alcatraz was to report the "escape" of their entire prison populations.

Police officers in every major city were being frantically urged to remain on duty.

Queen Elizabeth, in a memorable speech, exhorted all citizens of the Empire to remain calm and meet whatever might come with dignity, fortitude and honor.

The Scots stole the Stone of Scone again.

Rioting and looting began in Paris, Marseille, Barcelona, Milan, Amsterdam, Munich, Berlin.

The Pope was silent.

Turkey declared war on Syria and Iraq; peace was concluded a record three hours later.

On the 10th, Warsaw Radio announced the formation of a new Polish Provisional Government whose first and second acts had been, respectively, to abrogate all existing treaties with the Soviet Union and border states, and to petition the UN for restoration of the 1938 boundaries.

On the 11th East Germany, Austria, Czechoslovakia, Hungary, Romania, Bulgaria, Latvia and Lithuania followed suit, with variations on the boundary question.

On the 12th, after a brief but by no means bloodless putsch, the Spanish Republic was re-established; the British government fell once and the French government twice; and the Vatican issued a sharp protest against the ill-treatment of priests and nuns by Spanish insurgents.

Not a shot had been fired in Indo-China since the morning of the 8th.

On the 13th the Karelo-Finnish S. S. R., the Estonian S. S. R., the Byelorussian S. S. R., the Ukrainian S. S. R., the Azerbaijan S. S. R., the Turkmen S. S. R., and the Uzbek S. S. R. declared their independence of the Soviet Union. A horde of men and women escaped or released from forced-labor camps, the so-called Slave Army, poured westward out of Siberia.

VI

On the 14th, Zebulon, Georgia (pop. 312), Murfreesboro, Tennessee (pop. 11,190) and Orange, Texas (pop. 8,470) seceded from the Union.

That might have been funny, but on the 15th petitions for a secession referendum were circulating in Tennessee, Arkansas, Louisiana and South Carolina. Early returns averaged 61% in favor.

On the 16th Texas, Oklahoma, Mississippi, Alabama, Kentucky, Virginia, Georgia and—incongruously—Rhode Island and Minnesota added themselves to the list. Separatist fever was rising in Quebec, New Brunswick, Newfoundland and Labrador. Across the Atlantic, Catalonia, Bavaria, Moldavia, Sicily and Cyprus declared themselves independent states.

And that might have been hysteria. But that wasn't all.

Liquor stores and bars were sprouting like mushrooms in dry states. Ditto gambling halls, horse rooms, houses of prostitution, cockpits, burlesque theaters.

Moonshine whisky threatened for a few days to become the South's major industry, until standard-brand distillers cut their prices to meet the competition. Not a bottle of the new stocks of liquor carried a Federal tax stamp.

Mexican citizens were walking across the border into Arizona and New Mexico, swimming into Texas. The first shipload of Chinese arrived in San Francisco on the 16th.

Meat prices had increased by an average of sixty per cent for every day since the new control and rationing law took effect. By the 16th, round steak was selling for $10.80 a pound.

Resignations of public officials were no longer news; a headline in the Portland *Oregonian* for August 15th read:

WILL STAY AT DESK, SAYS GOVERNOR.

It hit me hard.

But when I thought about it, it was obvious enough; it was such an elementary thing that ordinarily you never noticed it—that all governments, not just tyrannies, but *all* governments were based on violence, as currency was based on metal. You might go for months or years without seeing a silver dollar or a policeman; but the dollar and the policeman had to be there.

The whole elaborate structure, the work of a thousand years, was coming down. The value of a dollar is established by a promise to pay; the effectiveness of a law, by a threat to punish.

Even if there were enough jailers left, how could you put a man in jail if he had ten or twenty friends who didn't want him to go?

How many people were going to pay their income taxes next year, even if there was a government left to pay them to?

And who was going to stop the landless people from spilling over into the nations that had land to spare?

Aza-Kra said, "These things are not necessary to do."

I turned around and looked at him. He had been lying motionless for more than an hour in the hammock I had rigged for him at the end of the room; I had thought he was asleep.

It was raining outside. Dim, colorless light came through

the slotted window blinds and striped his body like a melted barber pole. Caught in one of the bars of light, the tips of two quivering neck-spines glowed in faint filigree against the shadow.

"All right," I said. "Explain this one away. I'd like to hear you. Tell me why we don't need governments any more."

"The governments you have now—the governments of nations—they are not made for use. They exist to fight other nations."

"That's not true."

"It is true. Think. Of the money your government spends in a year, how much is for war and how much for use?"

"About sixty per cent for war. But that doesn't—"

"Please. This is sixty per cent now, when you have only a small war. When you have a large war, how much then?"

"Ninety per cent. Maybe more, but that hasn't got anything to do with it. In peace *or* wartime there are things a national government does that can't be done by anybody else. Now ask me for instance, what."

"Yes. I ask this."

"For instance, keeping an industrial country from being dragged down to coolie level by unrestricted immigration."

"You think it is better for those who have much to keep apart from those who have little, and give no help?"

"In principle, no, but it isn't just that easy. What good does it do the starving Asiatics if we turn America into another piece of Asia and starve along with them?"

He looked at me unwinkingly.

"What good has it done to keep apart?"

I opened my mouth, and shut it again. Last time it had been Japan, an island chain a little smaller than California. In the next one, half the world would have been against us.

"The problem is not easy, it is very difficult. But to solve it by helping is possible. To solve it by doing nothing is not possible."

"Harbors," I said. "Shipping. Soil conservation. Communications. Flood control."

"You do not believe these things can be done if there are no nations?"

"No. We haven't got time enough to pick up all the pieces. It's a hell of a lot easier to knock things apart than to put them together again."

"Your people have done things more difficult than this. You do not believe now, but you will see it done."

After a moment I said, "We're supposed to become a member of your galactic union now. Now that you've pulled our teeth. Who's going to build the ships?"

"Those who build them now."

I said, "Governments build them now."

"No. Men build ships. Men invent ships and design ships. Government builds nothing but more government."

I put my fists in my pockets and walked over to the window. Outside, a man went hurrying by in the rain, one hand at his hat-brim, the other at his chest. He didn't look around as he passed; his coffee-brown face was intent and impersonal. I watched him until he turned the corner, out of sight.

He had never heard of me, but his life would be changed by what I had done. His descendants would know my name; they would be bored by it in school, or their mothers would frighten them with it after dark.

Aza-Kra said, "To talk of these things is useless. If I would lie, I would not tell you that I lie. And if I would lie about these things, I would lie well, you would not find the truth by questions. You must wait. Soon you will know."

I looked at him. "When your friends come."

"Yes," he said.

And the feathery tips of his neck-spines delicately trembled.

They came on the last day of August—fifty great rotiform ships drifting down out of space. No radar spotted them; no planes or interceptor rockets went up to meet them. They followed the terminator around, landing at dawn; thirteen in the Americas, twenty-five in Europe and Asia, five in Africa, one each in England, Scandinavia, Australia, New Zealand, New Guinea, the Philippines, Japan.

Each one was six hundred feet across, but they rested lightly. Where they landed on sloping ground, slender curved supporting members came out of the doughnut-shaped rim, as dainty as insect's legs, and the fat lozenge of the hub lowered itself on the five fat spokes until it touched the earth.

Their doors opened.

In twenty-four days I had watched the nations of the Earth melt into shapelessness like sculptures molded of silicone putty. Armies, navies, air forces, police forces lost their cohesion first. In the beginning there were individual desertions, atoms escaping one at a time from the mass; later, when the pay failed to arrive, when there were no orders or else orders that could not be executed, men and women simply went home, orderly, without haste, in thousands.

Every useful item of equipment that could be carried or driven or flown went with them. Tractors, trucks, jeeps, bulldozers gladdened the hearts of farmers from Keokuk to Kweiyang. Bombers, small boats, even destroyers and battleships were in service as commercial transports. Quartermasters' stores were carried away piecemeal or in ton lots. Guns and ammunition rusted undisturbed.

Stock markets crashed. Banks failed. Treasuries failed. National governments broke down into states, provinces, cantons. In the United States, the President resigned his office on the 18th and left the White House, whose every window had been broken and whose lawn was newly landscaped with eggshells and orange rind. The Vice President resigned the next day, leaving the Presidency, in theory, to the Speaker of the House; but the Speaker was at home on his Arkansas farm; Congress had adjourned on the 17th.

Everywhere it was the same. The new governments of Asia and Eastern Europe, of Spain and Portugal and Argentina and Iran, died stillborn.

The Moon colonies had been evacuated; work had stopped on the Mars rocket. The men on duty in the orbital stations, after an anxious week, had reached an agreement for mutual disarmament and had come down to Earth.

Seven industries out of ten had closed down. The dollar was worth half a penny, the pound sterling a little more; the ruble, the Reichsmark, the franc, the sen, the yen, the rupee were waste paper.

The great cities were nine-tenths deserted, gutted by fires, the homes of looters, rats and roaches.

Even the local governments, the states, the cantons, the counties, the very townships, were too fragile to stand. All the arbitrary lines on the map had lost their meaning.

You could not say any more, "Japan will—" or "India is moving toward—" It was startling to realize that; to have to think of a sprawling, amorphous, unfathomable mass of infinitely varied human beings instead of a single inclusive symbol. It made you wonder if the symbol had ever had any connection with reality at all; whether there had ever been such a thing as a nation.

Toward the end of the month, I thought I saw a flicker of hope. The problem of famine was being attacked vigorously and efficiently by the Red Cross, the Salvation Army, and thousands of local volunteer groups: they commandeered fleets of trucks, emptied warehouses with a calm disregard of legality, and distributed the food where it was most needed. It was not enough—too much food had been destroyed and wasted by looters, too much had spoiled through neglect, and too much had been destroyed in the field by wandering, half-starved bands of the homeless—but it was a beginning; it was something.

Other groups were fighting the problem of these wolf-packs, with equally encouraging results. Farmers were forming themselves into mutual-defense groups, "communities of force." Two men could take any property from one man of equal strength without violence, without the penalty of pain; but not from two men, or three men.

One district warned the next when a wolf-pack was on the way, and how many to expect. When the pack converged on a field or a storehouse, men in equal or greater numbers were there to stand in the way. If the district could absorb, say, ten workers, that many of the pack were offered the option of staying; the rest had to move on. Gradually, the packs thinned.

In the same way, factories were able to protect themselves from theft. By an extension of the idea, even the money problem began to seem soluble. The old currency was all but worthless, and an individual's promise to pay in kind was no better as a medium of exchange; but promissory notes obligating whole communities could and did begin to circulate. They made an unwieldy currency, their range was limited, and they depreciated rapidly. But it was something, it was a beginning.

Then the wheel-ships came.

In every case but one, they were cautious. They landed in conspicuous positions, near a city or a village, and in the dawn light, before any man had come near them, oddly-shaped things came out and hurriedly unloaded boxes and bales, hundreds, thousands, a staggering array. They set up sun-reflecting beacons; then the ships rose again and disappeared, and when the first men came hesitantly out to investigate, they found nothing but the beacon, the acre of carefully-stacked boxes, and the signs, in the language of the country, that said:

THIS FOOD IS SENT BY THE PEOPLES OF OTHER WORLDS TO HELP YOU IN YOUR NEED. ALL MEN ARE BROTHERS.

And a brave man would lift the top of a box; inside he would see other boxes, and in them oblong pale shapes wrapped in something transparent that was not cellophane. He would unwrap one, feel it, smell it, show it around, and finally taste it; and then his eyebrows would go up.

The color and the texture were unfamiliar, but the taste was unmistakable. Tortillas and beans! (Or taro; or rice with beansprouts, or stuffed grape leaves, or herb omelette!)

The exception was the ship that landed outside Capetown, in an open field at the foot of Table Mountain.

Aza-Kra woke me at dawn. "They are here."

I mumbled at him and tried to turn over. He shook my shoulder again, buzzing excitedly to himself. "Please, they are here. We must hurry."

I lurched out of bed and stood swaying. "Your friends?" I said.

"Yes, yes." He was struggling into the black dress, pushing the peaked hat backward onto his head. *"Hurry."*

I splashed cold water on my face and got into my clothes.

I pulled out the top dresser drawer and looked at the two loaded automatics. I couldn't decide. I couldn't figure out any way they would do me any good, but I didn't want to leave them behind. I stood there until my legs went numb before I could make up my mind to take them anyhow, and the hell with it.

There were no taxis, of course. We walked three blocks along the deserted streets until we saw a battered sedan nose into view in the intersection ahead, moving cautiously around the heaps of litter.

"Hold your breath!"

The car moved on out of sight. We found it around the corner, up on the sidewalk with the front fender jammed against a railing. There were two men and a woman in it, Europeans.

"Which way?"

"Left. To the mountain."

When we got to the outskirts and the buildings began to thin out, I saw it up ahead, a huge silvery-metal shelf jutting out impossibly from the slope. I began to tremble. *They'll cut me up and put me in a jar,* I thought. *Now is the time to stop, if I'm going to.*

But I kept going. Where the road veered away from the field and went curving on up the mountain the other way, I stopped and we got out. I saw dark shapes and movements under that huge gleaming bulk. We stepped over a broken fence and started across the dry, uneven clods in the half-light.

Light sprang out: a soft, pearl-gray shimmer that didn't dazzle the eye although it was aimed straight toward us, marking the way. I heard a shrill wordless buzzing, and above that an explosion of chirping, and under them both a confusion of other sounds, humming, droning, clattering. I saw a half-dozen nightmare shapes bounding forward.

Two of them were like Aza-Kra; two more were squat things with huge humped shells on top, like tortoise-shells the size of a card table, with six long stump-ended legs underneath, and a tangle of eyes, tentacles, and small wriggly things peeping out in front; one, the tallest, had a long sharp-spined column of a body rising from a thick base and four startlingly human legs, and surmounted by four long whiplike tentacles and a smooth oval head; the sixth looked at first glance like an unholy cross between a grasshopper and a newt.

They crowded around Aza-Kra, humming, chirping, droning, buzzing, clattering. Their hands and tentacles went over him, caressingly; the newt-grasshopper thing hoisted him onto its back.

They paid no attention to me, and I stayed where I was with my hands tight and sweating on the grips of my guns. Then I heard Aza-Kra speak, and the tallest one turned back to me.

It reeked; something like brine, something like wet fur, something rank and indescribable. It had two narrow red eyes in that smooth knob of a head. It put one of its tentacles on my shoulder, and I didn't see a mouth open anywhere, but a droning voice said. "Thank you for caring for him. Come now. We go to ship."

I pulled away instinctively, quivering, and my hands came out of my pockets. I heard a flat, echoing *crack* and a yell, and I saw a red wetness spring out across the smooth skull; I saw the thing topple and lie in the dirt, twitching.

I thought for an instant that I had done it, the shot, the yell and all. Then I heard another yell, behind me: I whirled around and heard a car grind into gear and saw it bouncing away down the road into town, lights off, a black moving shape on the dimness. I saw it veer wildly and slew into the fence at the first turn; I heard its tires popping as it went through and the muffled crash as it turned over.

Dead, I thought. But the next time I looked I saw two figures come erect beyond the overturned car and stagger toward the road. They disappeared around the turn, running.

I looked back at the others, bewildered. They weren't even looking that way; they were gathered around the body, lifting it, carrying it toward the ship.

The feeling—the black depression that had been getting stronger every day for three weeks—tightened down on me as if somebody had turned a screw. I gritted my teeth against it, and stood there wishing I were dead.

They were almost to that open hatch in the oval hub that hung under the rim when Aza-Kra detached himself from the group and walked slowly back to me. After a moment one of the others—a hump-shelled one—trundled along after him and waited a yard or two away.

"It is not your fault," said Aza-Kra. "We could have prevented it, but we were careless. We were so glad to meet that we did not take precautions. It is not your fault. Come to the ship."

The hump-shelled thing came up and squeaked something, and Aza-Kra sat on its back. The tentacles waved at me. It wheeled and started toward the hatchway. "Come," said Aza-Kra.

I followed them, too miserable to care what happened. We went down a corridor full of the sourceless pearl-gray light until a doorway suddenly appeared, somehow, and we went through that into a room where two tripeds were waiting.

Aza-Kra climbed onto a stool, and one of the tripeds began pressing two small instruments against various parts of his body; the other squirted something from a flexible canister into his mouth.

And as I stood there watching, between one breath and the next, the depression went away.

I felt like a man whose toothache has just stopped; I probed at my mind, gingerly, expecting to find that the feeling was still there, only hiding. But it wasn't. It was gone so completely that I couldn't even remember exactly what it had been like. I felt calm and relaxed—and safe.

I looked at Aza-Kra. He was breathing easily; his eyes looked clearer than they had a moment before, and it seemed to me that his skin was glossier. The feathery neck-spines hung in relaxed, graceful curves.

. . . It was all true, then. It had to be. If they had been conquerors, the automatic death of the man who had killed one of their number, just now, wouldn't have been enough. An occupying army can never be satisfied with an eye for an eye. There must be retaliation.

But they hadn't done anything; they hadn't even used the

gas. They'd seen that the others in the car were running away, that the danger was over, and that ended it. The only emotions they had shown, as far as I could tell, were concern and regret—

Except that, I remembered now, I had seen two of the tripeds clearly when I turned back to look at them gathering around the body: Aza-Kra and another one. And their neck-spines had been stiff. . . .

Suddenly I knew the answer.

Aza-Kra came from a world where violence and cruelty didn't exist. To him, the Earth was a jungle—and I was one of its carnivores.

I knew, now, why I had felt the way I had for the last three weeks, and why the feeling had stopped a few minutes ago. My hostility toward him had been partly responsible for his fear, and so I had picked up an echo of it. Undirected fear is, by definition, anxiety, depression, uneasiness—the psychologists' *Angst*. It had stopped because Aza-Kra no longer had to depend on me; he was with his own people again; he was safe.

I knew the reason for my nightmares.

I knew why, time and again when I had expected Aza-Kra to be reading my mind, I had found that he wasn't. He did it only when he had to; it was too painful.

And one thing more:

I knew that when the true history of this time came to be written, I needn't worry about my place in it. My name would be there, all right, but nobody would remember it once he had shut the book.

Nobody would use my name as an insulting epithet, and nobody would carve it on the bases of any statues, either.

I wasn't the hero of the story.

It was Aza-Kra who had come down alone to a planet so deadly that no one else would risk his life on it until he had softened it up. It was Aza-Kra who had lived for nearly a month with a suspicious, irrational, combative, uncivilized flesh-eater. It was Aza-Kra who had used me, every step of the way—used my provincial loyalties and my self-interest and my prejudices.

He had done all that, weary, tortured, half-starved . . . and he'd been scared to death the whole time.

We made two stops up the coast and then moved into Algeria and the Sudan: landing, unloading, taking off again, following the dawn line. The other ships, Aza-Kra explained, would keep on circling the planet until enough food had been distributed to prevent any starvation until the next harvests. This one was going only as far as the middle of the North American continent—to drop me off. Then it was going to take Aza-Kra home.

I watched what happened after we left each place, in a vision device they had. In some places there was more hesitation than in others, but in the end they always took the food: in jeep-loads, by pack train, in baskets balanced on their heads.

Some of the repeaters worried me. I said, "How do you know it'll get distributed to everybody who needs it?"

I might have known the answer: "They will distribute it. No man can let his neighbor starve while he has plenty."

The famine relief was all they had come for, this time. Later, when we had got through the crisis, they would come back; and by that time, remembering the food, people would be more inclined to take them on their merits instead of shuddering because they had too many eyes or fingers. They would help us when we needed it, they would show us the way up the ladder, but we would have to do the work ourselves.

He asked me not to publish the story of Chillicothe and the month we had spent together. "Later, when it will hurt no one, you can explain. Now there is no need to make anyone ashamed; not even the officials of your government. It was not their fault; they did not make the planet as it was."

So there went even that two-bit chance at immortality.

It was still dawn when we landed on the bluff across the river from my home; sky and land and water were all the same depthless cool gray, except for the hairline of scarlet in the east. Dew was heavy on the grass, and the air had a smell that made me think of wood smoke and dry leaves.

He came out of the ship with me to say good-by.

"Will you be back?" I asked him.

He buzzed wordlessly in a way I had begun to recognize; I think it was his version of a laugh. "I think not for a very long time. I have already neglected my work too much."

"This isn't your work—opening up new planets?"

"No. It is not so common a thing, that a race becomes ready for space travel. It has not happened anywhere in the galaxy for twenty thousand of your years. I believe, and I hope, that it will not happen again for twenty thousand more. No, I am ordinarily a maker of—you have not the word, it is like porcelain, but a different material. Perhaps some day you will see a piece that I have made. It is stamped with my name."

He held out his hand and I took it. It was an awkward grip; his hand felt unpleasantly dry and smooth to me, and I suppose mine was clammy to him. We both let go as soon as we decently could.

Without turning, he walked away from me up the ramp. I said. "Aza-Kra!"

"Yes?"

"Just one more question. The galaxy's a big place. What happens if you miss just one bloodthirsty race that's ready to boil out across the stars—or if nobody has the guts to go and do to them what you did to us?"

"Now you begin to understand," he said. "That is the question the people of Mars asked us about you . . . twenty thousand years ago."

The story ends there, properly, but there's one more thing I want to say.

When Aza-Kra's ship lifted and disappeared, and I walked down to the bottom of the bluff and across the bridge into the city, I knew I was going back to a life that would be a lot different from the one I had known.

For one thing, the *Herald-Star* was all but done for when I came home: wrecked presses, half the staff gone, supplies running out. I worked hard for a little over a year trying to revive it, out of sentiment, but I knew there were more important things to be done than publishing a newspaper.

Like everybody else, I got used to the changes in the world and in the people around me: to the peaceful, un-worried feel of places that had been electric with tension; to the kids—the wonderful, incredible kids; to the new kind of excitement, the excitement that isn't like the night before execution, but like the night before Christmas.

But I hadn't realized how much I had changed, myself, until something that happened a week ago.

I'd lost touch with Eli Freeman after the paper folded; I knew he had gone into pest control, but I didn't know where he was or what he was doing until he turned up one day on the wheat-and-dairy farm I help run, south of the Platte in what used to be Nebraska. He's the advance man for a fleet of spray planes working out of Omaha, aborting rabbits.

He stayed on for three days, lining up a few of the stiff-necked farmers in this area that don't believe in hormones or airplanes either; in his free time he helped with the har-vest, and I saw a lot of him.

On his last night we talked late, working up from the old times to the new times and back again until there was noth-ing more to say. Finally, when we had both been quiet for a long time, he said something to me that is the only ac-colade I am likely to get, and oddly enough, the only one I want.

"You know, Bob, if it wasn't for that unique face of yours, it would be hard to believe you're the same guy I used to work for."

I said, "Hell, was I that bad?"

"Don't get shirty. You were okay. You didn't bleed the help or kick old ladies, but there just wasn't as much to you as there is now. I don't know," he said. "You're—more human."

More human.

Yes. We all are.

DOUBLE MEANING

SOMEWHERE IN THE CITY A MONSTER WAS HIDING.

Lying back against the limousine's cushions, Thorne Spangler let his mind dwell on that thought, absorbing it with the deliberate enjoyment of a small boy sucking a piece of candy. He visualized the monster, walking down a lighted street, or sitting in a cheap hired room, tentacles coiled, waiting, under the shell that made it look like a man—or a woman. And all around it, the life of the city going on: *Hello, Jeff. Have you heard? They're stopping all the cars. Some sort of spy case . . . My sister tried to fly out of Tucson, and they turned her back. My cousin at the spaceport says nothing is coming in or leaving except military ships. It must be something big.*

And the monster, listening, feeling the net tighten around it.

The tension was growing, Spangler thought; it hung in the air, in the abnormally empty streets. You could hear it: a stillness that welled up under the beehive hum—a waiting stillness, that made you want to stop and hold your breath.

Spangler glanced at Pembun, sitting quietly beside him. Does he feel it? he wondered. It was hard to tell. You never knew what a colonial was thinking. Probably, he decided, he's most heartily wishing himself back on his own sleepy planet, far from all this commotion at the hub of the Universe.

For Spangler himself, this moment was the climax of a lifetime. The monster—the Rithian—was only the catalyst, the stone flung into the pool. The salient fact was that just now, for as long as the operation lasted, all the interminable workings of the Earth Empire revolved around one tiny sphere: Earth Security Department, North American District, Southwestern Sector. For this brief time, one man, Spangler, was more important than all the others who administered the Empire.

The car decelerated smoothly and stopped. Two men in the pearl-gray knee breeches of the city patrol barred the way, both with automatic weapons at the ready. Behind them, the squat bulk of a Gun Unit covered half the roadway.

Two more patrolmen came forward and flung open all the doors of the car, stepping back smartly into crossfire positions. "All out," said the one with the sergeant's cape. "Security check. Move!"

As Spangler passed him, the sergeant touched his chest respectfully. "Good evening, Commissioner."

"Sergeant," said Spangler, in tranquil acknowledgment, smiling but not troubling himself to look at the man directly; and he led Pembun and the chauffeur to the end of the queue.

As the line moved on, Spangler turned and found Pembun craning his short neck curiously. "It's a stereoptic fluoroscope," Spangler explained with languid amusement. "That's one test the Rithian can't meet, no matter how good his human disguise may be. One of these check stations is set up at each corner of every tenth avenue and every fifth cross-street. If the Rithian is fool enough to pass one, we have him. If he doesn't, the house checks will force him out. He doesn't have a chance."

Spangler stepped between the screen and the bulbous twin projectors, and saw the glowing, three-dimensional image of his skeleton appear in the hooded screen. The square blotch at the left wrist and the smaller one near it were his communicator and thumb-watch. The other, odd-shaped ones lower down were metal objects in his belt pouch—key projectors, calculator, memocubes and the like.

The technician perched above the projector said. "Turn around. All right. Next."

Spangler waited at the limousine door until Pembun joined him. The little man's wide, flat-nosed face expressed surprise, interest, and something else that Spangler could not quite define.

" 'Ow did you ever get 'old of so many portable fluoroscopes in such a 'urry?" he asked.

Spangler smiled delightedly. "It's no miracle, Mr. Pembun, just adequate preparation. Those scopes have been stored and maintained, for exactly this emergency, since twenty eighteen."

"Five 'undred years," said Pembun wonderingly. "My! And this is the first time you've 'ad to use them?"

"The first time." Spangler waved Pembun into the car. Following him, he continued, "But it took just under half an hour to set up the complete network. Not only the fluoroscopes were ready, but complete, detailed plans of the entire operation. All I had to do was to take them out of the files."

The car moved forward past the barrier.

"My!" said Pembun again. "I feel kind of like an extra nose." His eyes gleamed faintly in the half-dark as Spangler turned to look at him.

"I beg your pardon?"

"I mean," said Pembun, "it doesn't seem to me as if you rilly need me very much."

That expressionless drawl, Spangler thought, could become irritating in time. The man had been educated on Earth; why couldn't he speak properly?

"I'm sure your advice will prove invaluable, Mr. Pembun," he said smoothly. "After all, we have no one here who's actually had . . . friendly contact with the Rithians."

"That's right," said Pembun, "I almost forgot. We're so used to the Rithi, ourselves, it's kind of 'ard to remember that Earth never did any trading with them." He pronounced "Rithi" with a curious whistling fricative, something between *th* and *s*, and an abrupt terminal vowel. It was not done for swank, Spangler thought; it simply came more naturally to the man than the Standardized "Rithians." Probably Pembun spoke the Rithian tongue at least as well as he spoke standard English.

Spangler half-heartedly tried to imagine himself a part of Pembun's world. A piebald rabble, spawned by half a dozen substandard groups that had left Earth six centuries before. Haitians, French West Africans, Jamaicans, Puerto Ricans. Low-browed, dull-eyed loafers, breeders, drinkers and brawlers, speaking an unbelievable tongue corrupted from already degraded English, French and Spanish. *Colonials*— in fact, if not in name.

"We couldn't do any trading with the Rithians, Mr. Pembun," he said at last, softly. "They are not human."

"Yes, I recollec' now, Commissioner," the little man replied humbly. "It jus' slipped my mind for a minute. Shoo, I was taught about that in school. Earth's 'ad the same policy toward non-'uman cultures for the last five 'undred years. If they 'aven't got to the spaceship stage yet, put them under surveillance and make sure they don't. If they 'ave, and they're weak enough, give them a quick preventive war. If they're too strong, like the Rithi—delaying tactics, subversion, sabotage, divide-and-rule. *Then* war." He chuckled. "It makes my 'ead ache jus' thinking about it."

"That policy," Spangler informed him, "has withstood the only meaningful test. Earth survives."

"Yes, sir," said Pembun vacuously. "She certainly does."

The things, Spangler thought half in mockery, half in real annoyance, that I do for the Empire!

A touch of his forefinger at the base of the square, jeweled thumbwatch produced a soft chime and then a female voice: "Fourteen-ten and one quarter."

Spangler hesitated. It was an awkward time to call Joanna; the afternoon break, in her section, came at fourteen thirty. But if he waited until then he would be back at the Hill himself, tied up in a conference that might not end until near quitting time. It was irritating to have to speak to her in Pembun's presence, too, but there was no help for it now. He had been too busy to call earlier in the afternoon—Pembun's arrival had upset his schedule—and his superior, Keith-Ingram, had chosen to call him while he was on the way to the spaceport, occupying the whole journey with fruitless discussion.

He had not called her for three days. That had been deliberate; this Rithian business was only a convenient pretext. It was good strategy. But Spangler knew his antagonist, knew the limits of her curiosity and pride almost to the hour. Any longer delay would be dangerous.

Spangler reached for the studs of the limousine's communicator, set into the front wall of the compartment. His wrist-phone would have been easier and more private, but he wanted to see her face.

"You'll excuse me?" he said perfunctorily.

"Of cawse." The little man turned toward the window of his side of the car, presenting his back to Spangler and the communicator screen.

Spangler punched the number. After a moment the screen lighted and Joanna's face came into view.

"Oh—Thorne."

Her tone was poised, cool, almost expressionless—that was to say, normal. She looked at him, out of the screen's upholstered frame, with the expression that almost never changed; direct, gravely intent, receptive. Her skin and eyes were so clear, her emotional responses so deliberate and pallid that she seemed utterly, almost abstractly normal: a type personified, a symbol, a mathematical fiction. Everything about her was refined and subdued: her gestures, movements, her rare laughter. Her face itself might have been modeled to fit the average man's notion of "aristocracy."

That, of course, was why Spangler had to have her.

In this one respect, she was precisely what she looked—the Planters were one of the oldest, most powerful, and most unassailably patrician families in the Empire. Without such an alliance, Spangler knew painfully well, he had gone as far as he could, and a good deal farther than a less determined man could have hoped. With her, he would only have begun—and his children would receive, by right of birth, all that he had struggled to gain.

In nearly all other ways, Joanna was a mirror of deception. She seemed cool and self-possessed, but was neither; she was only afraid. It was fear that delayed and censored every word she spoke, every motion: fear of betraying herself, fear of demanding too much, fear of giving too much.

He let the silence lengthen until, in another second, it would have been obvious that he was hesitating for effect. Then he said politely, "I'm not disturbing you?"

". . . No, of course not." The pause before she answered had been a trifle longer than normal.

She's hurt, Spangler thought with satisfaction.

"I would have called earlier, if I could," he said soberly. "This is the first free moment I've had in three days."

It was a lie, and she knew it; but it was so near the truth that she could accept it, if she chose, without loss of dignity. That was the knife-edge on which Spangler had hung his fortunes. Deliberately, knowing the risk, he had drawn their relationship so thin that a touch would break it.

Had there been any other course he could have taken? Despite himself, Spangler's anxiety led him through each stage of the logic again, searching for a flaw.

Cancel the approach direct. He had asked her to marry him, for the first time, a week after they had become lovers. She had refused without hesitation and without coyness; she meant it.

Cancel the approach dialectical. Joanna had a keen and capable mind, but she could be as stubborn as any dullard. There is no argument that will wear down a woman's "I don't want to."

Cancel the approach violent: tentatively. Four days ago, at the end of a long weekend they had spent together in the Carpathians, he had tried brutality—not on impulse, but with calculated design which had achieved its primary object: he had reduced her to tears.

After that, apology and reconciliation. After that, silence: three days of it. Silence wounds more that a blow, and wounds more deeply.

Joanna had spent her whole life in retreating from things which had injured her.

But Spangler had three things on his side: Joanna's affection and need for him; ordinary human perversity, which desires a thing, however often refused, the instant it is withdrawn; and the breaking of the rhythm. Rhythm, however desirable in some aspects of the relations between sexes, is fatal in most others. Request, argument, violence— If he had begun the cycle again, as both of them subconsciously expected, he would simply have made his own defeat more certain.

As it was, he had weakened her resistance by making her gather it against a thrust that never came. . . .

Joanna said, "I understand. You do look tired, Thorne. You're all right, though, aren't you?"

Spangler said abruptly, "Joanna, I want to see you. Soon. Tonight. Will you meet me?"

Before, his tone had been almost as casual as hers, and he had watched the minuscule change in her expression that meant she was softening toward him. Now he spoke urgently, and saw her stiffen again.

Never let her rest, he thought. Never let her get her balance. . . . He spoke softly again: "It will be the last time, if you decide it that way. But let me see you tonight."

". . . All right."

"Shall I send a car for you?"

She nodded, and then her image dissolved. Spangler leaned back, with a sigh, into the cushions.

"My," said Pembun. "Look at awl the tawl buildings!"

They were stopped twice more before they reached Administration Hill, and went through a routine search at the entrance. From there, the trip to Security Section took less than a minute. The chauffeur left them at Spangler's office door and took the limousine to the motor pool three levels below.

Contrasted with the group that was waiting at the conference table, under the hard, clear glow-light, Pembun looked like a shabby mongrel that had somehow crawled into the purebred kennel. His skin was yellowish under the brown;

his jowls were wider than his naked cranium; his enormous ears stuck out straight from his head. His tunic and pantaloons were correctly cut, but he looked hopelessly awkward in them.

After all, Spangler reminded himself carefully, the man could not help being what he was.

"Gentlemen," he said, "allow me to present Mr. Jawj Pembun of Manhaven. Mr. Pembun was a member of the colonial government before his planet gained its independence, and since that time has been of service to the Empire in various capacities. He brings us expert knowledge of the Rithians. Lieutenant Colonel Cassina, who is our liaison with the Space Navy—his new aide, Captain Wei—Dr. Baustian of the Bureau of Alien Physiology—Mr. Pemberton of the Mayor's staff—Miss Timoney and Mr. Gordon, of this office."

Pembun shook hands with all of them without any noticeable sign of awe. To the Mayor's spokesman he said affably, "You know, Pemberton was origin'ly my family's name. They just gradually shortened it to Pembun. That's a coincidence, isn't it?"

Pemberton, a fine-boned young man with pale eyes and hair, stiffened visibly.

"I hardly think there is any relation," he said.

Spangler picked up a memo spool that lay beside him and tapped it sharply against the table. "At the suggestion of the Foreign Relations Department," he said delicately, "Mr. Pembun was brought in from Ganymede especially for this emergency. I arranged for his passage through the cordon and met him personally at the spaceport." In short, gentlemen, he thought, this incredible little man has been wished on us by the powers that be, and we shall have to put up with him as best we can.

"Now," he said, "I imagine Mr. Pembun would like to be brought up to date before we proceed." There was a snort from Colonel Cassina which Spangler pointedly ignored. He began the story, covering the main points quickly and concisely. Pembun stopped him only once to ask a question.

"Are you sure that's all the Rithi there were to begin with—just seven?"

"No, Mr. Pembun," Spangler admitted. "We don't yet know how or by whom they were smuggled through to Earth, therefore we must consider the possibility that others are still undetected. To deal with that possibility, Security is patrolling the entire planet, using a random-based spot check system. But we know that these seven were here, and that one of them is still at large. When we find him, we hope to get all the information we need. The idea of suicide is repugnant to these Rithians, I understand."

"That's right," said Pembun soberly. "I guess you can take him alive, all right. Prob'ly could 'ave taken all seven after the accident, if your patrolmen 'adn' shot so quick."

"Those were city patrolmen," said Pemberton acidly, with a flush on his cheekbones, "not Security men. Their conduct was perfectly in order. When they arrived on the scene of the accident, and saw three men attempting to aid four others whose bodies were torn open, exposing the alien shapes underneath, they instantly fired on the whole group. Those were their orders; that was what they had been trained to do in any such event. They would have been right, even if one of the Rithians had not escaped into the crowd."

Pembun shook his head, smiling. "I'm not so good at paradoxes," he said. "They jus' mix me up."

"There is no paradox, Mr. Pembun," said Spangler gently. "A fully equipped Security crew can take chances with an unknown force which a municipal patrol cannot. A patrolman discovering an alien on this planet must kill first and investigate afterwards—because an alien spy or saboteur, by definition, has unknown potentialities. Planning centuries in advance, as we must, we obviously can't foresee every possible variant of a basic situation; but we can and do lay down directives which will serve our best interests in the vast majority of cases. And we can't, Mr. Pembun, we can*not* allow crucial decisions to be made on the spot by non-executive personnel."

Colonel Cassina cleared his throat impatiently. "Shall we get on?"

"Just one moment. Mr. Pembun, I want to make this

point clear to you if I can. *Interpretation is the dry rot of law.* One interpretation, and the law is modified; two, the law is distorted—three hundred million, and there is no law at all, there is pure anarchy. In a small system, of course—a single planet, for example—there are only a few intermediate stages between planning and execution. But when you consider that we're dealing here with an empire of two hundred sixty planets, an aggregate of more than *eight hundred billion* people, you'll realize that directives must be rigid and policy unified. In an emergency, the lower-echelon official who acts according to his own personal interpretation may be right or wrong. The similar official who follows a rigid policy, prepared to meet the widest possible variety of actual situations, *will* be right—in ninety-nine point nine out of a hundred cases. We take the long view: we can't afford to do otherwise.''

Pembun nodded seriously. He said, ''We 'ad the same trouble at 'ome—on a smaller scale, of course. Right after we declared our independence, we formed a federation with the two other planets in our system, Novaya Zemlya and Reunion. It seemed like a good idea—you know, for mutual defense and so on. But we found out to keep that big a gover'ment running we 'ad to stiffen it up something dreadful, an' some'ow or other it didn't seem to be as cheap to run as three diff'rent gover'ments, either. So we split up ag'in.''

Spangler kept his urbane expression with difficulty. Colonel Cassina's neck was brick red, and Dr. Baustian, Captain Wei and Miss Timoney were staring at Pembun in frank amazement. The others looked embarrassed.

Really, it was a waste of time to take any pains with a barbarian like this. Try to explain the philosophy behind the workings of the greatest empire in history, and all Pembun got out of it was a childish analogy to the history of his own pipsqueak solar system!

He regarded the little man through narrowed lids. Come to think of it, was Pembun really as simple as he appeared, or was he snickering to himself behind that stolid yellow-brown face?

He had said several things which could only be explained

by the worst of bad taste or the sheerest blind ignorance. After Spangler's reference to Manhaven's "gaining its independence"—surely a polite way of putting it, since Manhaven had seceded from the Empire only on Earth's sufferance, at a time when she was occupied elsewhere— Pembun had said, "After we *declared* our independence—"

Carelessness, or deliberate, subtly pointed insult?

Was Pembun saying, "There are two hundred sixty planets and eight hundred billion people in your Empire, all right—but there used to be a lot more, and a century from now there'll be a lot less"?

Insufferable little planet-crawler . . .

Colonel Cassina said, "Mr. Pembun, do I understand you to suggest that we too should *split up* as you put it? That the Empire should be *liquidated*?"

"Why, no, Colonel," said Pembun. "That wouldn' be any business of mine, you know. That would be up to the people that still live in the Empire to decide."

Cassina snorted and sputtered. Pemberton's face was white with indignation. It was remarkable, Spangler thought with one corner of his mind, how easily Pembun was able to rub them all the wrong way. If it could possibly be arranged, future conferences had better be held without him.

"Gentlemen," he said, raising his voice a trifle, "shall we continue?"

After they had left, Spangler sat alone in his inner office, absently toying with the buttons that controlled the big information screen opposite his desk. He switched on one organizational chart after another, without seeing any of them.

Pembun had behaved himself, in a manner of speaking, after that clash with Cassina. But the things he had said had become not merely irritating, but—disquieting.

It had started with the usual complaint from Pemberton, speaking for the mayor. Like almost every planetary and local government department except Security, the city administration wanted to know when the Rithian would be captured and the planet-wide blockade ended.

Spangler had assured him that the Rithian could not possibly remain concealed for more than a week at the utmost.

And then Pembun had remarked, "Excuse me, Commissioner, but I b'lieve it would be safer if you said two
months."

"*Why*, Mr. Pembun?"

"Well, becawse Rithi got to 'ave a lot of beryllium salts
in their food. The way I see it, this one Ritch wouldn' 'ave
more than six or eight weeks' supply with 'im. After that,
you can either tie up all the supplies of beryllium salts, so
'e 'as to surrender or starve, or jus' watch the chemical
supply 'ouses an' arrest anybody 'oo buys them. Either way,
you got 'im. Might take a little more than two months. Say
two and a 'alf or three."

"Mr. Pembun," Spangler said with icy patience, "that's
an admirable plan, but we're not going to need it. The house
checks will get our Rithian before a week is up."

"Clear ever'body out of a building, an' wawk them all
past one of those fluoroscopes?"

"That's it," Spangler told him. "One area at a time,
working inward from the outskirts of the city to the center."

"Uh-mm," said Pembun. "Only thing is, the Rithi got
no bones."

Spangler raised his brows and glanced at Dr. Baustian.
"Is that correct, doctor?"

"Well, yes, so I understand," said the physiologist tol-
erantly, "but I assume that would be indication enough—if
the fluoroscope showed a very small cartilage and no bones
at all?"

Laughter rippled around the table.

"Not," said Pembun, "if 'e swallowed a skel'ton."

Cassina said something rude in an explosive voice. Spangler, incredulous amusement bubbling up inside him, stared
at Pembun. "*Swallowed* a skeleton?"

"Uh-mm. You people wouldn't know 'bout it, I guess,
becawse you 'aven' done any trading with the Rithi—
scientific trading least of awl—but the Rithi got . . ." He
hesitated. "Our name for it is *mudabs boyó*; I guess in
Standard that would be 'protean insides.' "

"Protean!" from Dr. Baustian.

"Yes, sir. Their outside shape is fixed, almos' as much as ours, or they wouldn't need any disguises to look like a man; but the insides is pretty near all protean flesh—make it into a stomach, or a bowel, or a bladder, or w'atever they want. They could swallow a yuman skel'ton, all right—it wouldn' inconvenience them at awl. An' they could imitate the rest of a man's insides well enough to fool you. They could make it move natural, too. That means they wouldn' need any braces or anything, jus' a plastic shell for a disguise.

"I 'ate to say it, but I don' believe those fluoroscopes are going to do much good."

In a moment, the table had been in an uproar again.

Spangler grunted, switched on his speakwrite and began to dictate a report of the conference. "To Claude Keith-Ingram, Chief Comm DeptSecur," he said. "Most Secret. Most Urgent." He thought for a moment, then rapidly gave an account of Pembun's statement, adding that Dr. Baustian doubted the validity of his information, and that Pembun admitted he had never seen any actual evidence of the Rithians' alleged protean ability.

He read it over, then detached the spool and tossed it into the *out* tube.

He was still unsatisfied.

He had done everything he could be expected to do, exactly according to regulations. If policy were to be changed, it was not for him to change it. Logic and instinct both assured him that Pembun was not to be taken seriously.

But there was something else Pembun had said that still bothered him, for a reason he could not explain. He had not included it in his report; it would have seemed, to put it mildly, frivolous.

Pembun had said:

"There's one more thing you got to watch out for—those Rithi got a 'ell of a sense of yumor."

Spangler passed his hand over the intercom. "Gordon," he said.

"Yes, sir?"

"Did you find quarters for Mr. Pembun?"

"Yes, sir."

"Where is he?"

"G-level, section seven, Suite One-eleven."

"Right," said Spangler, flicking his hand over the intercom to break the connection. He stood up, walked out of the office, and buzzed a scooter.

"G-level," he said into its mechanical ear.

II

THE DOOR OF SUITE 111 WAS AJAR. INSIDE, A BARITONE
voice was singing to the accompaniment of some stringed
instrument. Spangler paused and listened.

Odum Páwkee mónt a mút-ting
Vágis cásh odúm Paw-kée
Odum Páwkee mónt a mút-ting
Tóuda por tásh o cáw-fée!

There was a final chord, then a hollow wooden thump
and jangle as the instrument was set down; then the clink
of ice cubes in a glass.

Spangler put his hand over the doorplate. The chime was
followed by Pembun's voice calling, "Come awn in!"

Pembun was comfortably slumped in a recliner, with his
collar undone and his feet high. The glass in his hand, judg-
ing by color, contained straight whiskey. On a low table at
his side were the remains of a man-sized meal, a decanter,
an ice bucket and several clean glasses, and the instrument—a tiny, round-bellied thing with three strings.

The little man swung himself lithely around and rose. "I

was 'oping somebody would cawl," he said happily. "Gets
kind of lonesome in this place—lonesomer than the mountings a thousand miles from anybody, some'ow. 'Ere, take
the company seat, Commissioner. A glawss of w'iskey?"

Spangler took an upright chair. "This will do nicely,"
he said. "No thanks to the whiskey—I haven't your stomach."

Pembun looked startled, then smiled. "I'll get them to
sen' up some soda," he said. He swung himself into the
recliner again, reached for the intercom and gave the order.

"W'y I looked surprised for a minute w'en you said
that," he explained, turning sidewise on the recliner, "is
becawse we got an expression on Man'aven. W'en we say,
'I aven' got your stomach,' that means I don' like you,
we're not sympathetic. *'E no ay to stomá.*"

Spangler felt an unexpected twinge of guilt—of course
Pembun knew he wasn't liked—and then a wave of irritation. Damn the man! How did he always manage to put one
in the wrong?

He kept his voice casual and friendly. "What was that
you were singing, just before I came in?"

"Oh, that—'Odum Pawkee Mont a Mutting.' " He
picked up the instrument and sang the chorus Spangler had
heard. Spangler listened, charmed in spite of himself. The
melody was simple and jaunty—the kind of thing, he told
himself, that would go well sung on muleback . . . or the
backs of whatever ill-formed beasts the Manhavenites used
instead of mules.

Pembun put the instrument down. "In English, that
means, 'Old Man Pawkey climbs a mounting, clouds 'ide
Old Man Pawkey. Old Man Pawkey climbs a mounting, all
for a cup of coffee!' "

"Is there more?"

Pembun made his eyes comically wide, "Oh, shoo!
There's 'bout a trillion verses. I only know every tenth one,
about, but we'd be 'ere all night if I sang 'em. It's kind of
a saga. Old Man Pawkey was a settler who lived up in the
Desperation Mountings in the early days. That's in the tem-
perate zone, but even so it's awful wild country, all straight
up and straight down. 'E loved coffee, but of course there

wasn' any. Well, 'e 'eard there was some in the spaceport town, Granpeer, down in the plateau country, and 'e went there, on foot. Twenty-two 'undred kilometers. Or so they say.''

The conveyor door popped open. Pembun went over to get the soda and pour Spangler a drink. "There were some big things done in those days," he added, "but there were some big lies told, too."

Spangler felt an obscure shock that made him jump again. In the conscious effort to sympathize with Pembun, to understand the man in his own terms, he had managed to build up a picture which was really not too hard to admire: the wild, colorful, free life of the frontier, the hardships accepted and conquered, the deeds of heroism casually done, et cetera, et cetera. And then Pembun himself, in half a sentence, had indifferently rejected that picture. "There were some big lies told, too."

Pembun didn't believe in the Empire; all right. But—if he had no respect for his own planet's traditions, then what in the name of sanity *did* he believe in?

Spangler was a man who tried hard to be liberal. But now, staring at Pembun's round brown face, the yellowish whites of his eyes, he thought once more: It's a waste of time to try to understand this man. He's not civilized: he thinks like an animal. There's simply *no point of contact*.

He said abruptly, "At the meeting, you mentioned something about the Rithians' 'sense of humor.' What, exactly, did you mean?"

He was thinking: In a few minutes I'll be back in my office. I'll drink half of this highball, precisely, and then go.

Pembun leaned back in the relaxer, head turned slightly, eyes alert on Spangler. "Well," he said, "they're kind of peculiar, in this way. They're a real 'ighly-advanced people, technologically—you know that. But the things that strike them funny remind you more of a kind of backwoods planet, like Man'aven. Maybe that's w'y we got along so well with them—Man'aven yumor is kind of primitive. Pulling out a chair we'n a man goes to sit down. That kind of thing. But they beat us.

"They'll go forty miles out of their way to play a joke, even w'en it isn' good business. I've 'eard a novel written by one of their big authors—twelve spools, mus' be more than five 'undred thousan' words long—jus' so 'e could build up to a dirty joke at the end. It was a bes'-seller in their solar system. An' they're crazy about puns—plays on words. Some of their sentences you're suppose' to read as many as fifteen, twenty different ways."

Spangler's memory groped uneasily for a moment and then produced a relevant fact from his training days. "Like Joyce," he said. "The twentieth-century decadent."

"Uh-mm," Pembun agreed. "I use' to be able to quote pages of *Finnegans Wake*: 'riverrun, past Eve and Adam's, from swerve of shore to bend of bay, brings us by a commodious vicus of recirculation . . .' That's primer talk, compared to Rithi literature."

Spangler swallowed deliberately and set his glass down on the wide arm of his chair. He felt the vast, cool, good-humored patience of a man who knows how to retreat from his own petty emotions. "I don't want to seem obtuse," he said, "but has this got anything to do with my problem?"

Pembun's brows creased delicately. He looked anxious, searching for words. "Nothing, *specifically*," he said earnestly. "W'at I mean is jus' that in general, you got to watch out for that sense of yumor. I mean, you already know that this Rithch is going to 'urt you bad if 'e can. But you got to remember also that if 'e can, 'e's going to do it some way that'll be sidesplittingly funny to 'im. It isn' easy to figure out w'ich way a Rithch is going to jump, but you can do it sometimes if you know w'at makes them lahf."

Spangler swallowed again, leaving exactly half the drink behind, and stood up. He was a trifle impatient with himself for having come here at all, but at least he had the satisfaction of knowing that a lead had been explored and canceled out, that an x had been corrected to a zero.

"Thank you, Mr. Pembun," he said from the doorway, "for the drink and the information. Good evening."

"You got to look out for the 'ypnotism, too," said Pembun as an afterthought.

Spangler stood in the doorway without speaking. Pembun looked at him with a politely inquiring expression.

"Hypnotism!" Spangler said, and started back into the room. "What hypnotism?"

"My goodness," cried Pembun, "didn' you know about *that*?"

They lay together in companionable silence, in a darkened room, facing the huge unscreened window—window in the archaic sense, a simple hole in the wall—through which the feather-light touch of cool, salt air came unhindered. On either side, where the shore thrust out an arm, Spangler could see a cluster of multicolored lights—Angels proper on the right, St. Monica on the left. Straight ahead was nothing but silver sea and ghost-gray cloud, except when the tiny spark of an airship crossed silently and was gone.

The universe was a huge, half-felt presence that flowed through the open window to contain them; as if, Spangler thought, they were two grains of dust sunk in an ocean that stretched to infinity.

It was soothing, in a way, but there was a touch of unpleasantness in it. Spangler shifted his body restlessly, feeling the breeze fumble at his bare skin. The scale was too big, he thought; he was too used to the rabbit-warren of the Hill, perhaps, to be entirely easy outside it. Perhaps he needed a change. . . .

"That wind is getting a little chilly," he said. "Let's close the window and turn on the lights."

"I thought it was nice," she said. "But go ahead, if you like." Now I've insulted her window, Spangler thought wryly. Nevertheless, he reached forward and found the stud that rolled a sheet of vitrin down over the opening.

It was a period piece, the window—21st century, even to the antique servo mechanism that operated it. So was everything else in Joanna's tower: the absurd four-legged chairs, the massive tables, the carpets, even the huge pneumatic couch. There were paper books in the shelves, and not the usual decorator's choices, either, but books that a well-read twenty-first-century citizen might actually have owned—Shakespeare and Sterne, Jones and Joyce, Homer

and Hemingway all jumbled in together. If the fashion would
let her, Spangler thought, I believe she would wear dresses.

A glow of rose-tinted light sprang up and he turned to
see Joanna with one slender arm around her knees, her head
bent solemnly over the lighted cigarette she had just taken
from the dispenser. She handed him another.

Spangler pulled himself up beside her and leaned against
the back of the couch. The smoke of their cigarettes fanned
out, pink in the half-light, and faded slowly into floating
haze.

The room's curved walls and ceiling enclosed them
snugly, safely. . . .

The 21st century, the Century of Peace, was a womb,
Spangler thought. The comment was Joanna's, not his; she
had picked it up in some book or other. "A womb with a
view." That was it. A childishly fanciful description, as one
would expect from that period, but accurate enough. Self-
deception was not one of Joanna's vices—unfortunately. To
win her finally and completely, it would be necessary to
break down the clear image she had of herself—cast her
adrift in chaos, so that she would turn blindly to him for
her lost security. It was not going to be easy.

Joanna said, without moving, "Thorne, I'd like to talk
seriously to you, just for a minute."

"Of course."

"You know what I'm going to say, probably; but just to
have things clear—Do you want us to go on together?"

Matching her tone, Spangler said, "Yes."

". . . I do too. You know I'm fonder of you than I've
ever been of anyone. But I won't ever marry you. You've
got to believe that, and accept it, or it's no good. . . . I'm
trying to be fair."

"You're succeeding," Spangler told her lightly. He turned
and put his hand on her knee. "Just to be equally clear—I've
been insufferable to you, and I was a maniac last weekend,
and I'm sorry for it. Shall we both forget it?"

She smiled. "Yes. We will."

Her lips moved and altered as he leaned toward her: cor-
ners turning downward, pink moist flesh swelling up into
the blind shape of desire. His free arm sank into the soft-

ness of her back, abruptly hard as her body tautened. Eyes closed, he heard the sibilant whisper of her legs slowly straightening against the counterpane.

Afterward, he lay wrapped in a warm lethargy that was like floating in quiet water. It was an effort to force himself out of that mindless content, but it was necessary. As he was vulnerable at this moment, so was she. When she spoke to him lazily, he answered her with increasing constraint, until he felt his tension flow into her.

Then he rolled over abruptly, got up and stood at the window, staring out at the vast, obscene emptiness of sky and sea. Now it was easier. As he had often, in his childhood, worked himself deliberately into white-hot anger—when, if he had not forced himself to be angry, he would have been afraid—now, with equal deliberateness, he opened his mind to despair.

Suppose that I failed, and lost Joanna, he thought. But that was not enough. What would be the most dreadful thing that could possibly happen? The answer came of itself; Pembun, and his Rithians with their boneless bodies and their hypnotism. Shapeless faces staring in from a sea of darkness. *Suppose they won.* Suppose the Empire went down under that insensate wave, and all the walls everywhere crumbled to let smothering Chaos in?

Her voice: "Thorne? Is anything the matter?"

He pulled himself back, shuddering, from the cold emptiness that his mind had fastened upon. For an instant it had been real, it had happened, it was *there*. He had been lost and alone, fumbling in an endless night.

When he turned, he knew that his agony showed plainly in his face. He did his best to restrain and suppress it: that would show too.

"Nothing," he said. He walked around the couch, reached past her for a cigarette, then moved to the closet.

"You're going?" she asked uncertainly.

"I've got to be in early tomorrow," he said. "And I've been going a little short of sleep."

". . . All right."

Fastening his cloak, he went to her and took her hand.

"Don't mind me, will you? I'm a little jumpy—it's been an unpleasant week. I'll call you tomorrow."

Her lips smiled, but her eyes were wide and unfocused. Caution was in them, and a hint of something else—pleasure, perhaps, touched with guilt?

He rode home with a feeling of satisfaction that deepened into a fierce joy. If she learned that she could hurt him, learned to expect it, learned to like it, then in time she would endure the thought of being hurt in return. It was only necessary to go slowly, advancing and retreating, shifting his ground, stripping her defenses gradually: until at last, whether for guilt or pleasure, or love, she would marry him.

For love and pleasure, fear and hatred, honor and ambition were all doors that could be opened or shut.

Pain was the key.

Early the following morning, alone in his inner office, Spangler sat composedly and looked into his desk screen, from which the broad gray face of Claude Keith-Ingram stared back at him.

"You asked Pembun why he hadn't divulged this information earlier?" Keith-Ingram demanded sharply.

"I did," Spangler said. "He answered that he had assumed we already knew it, since the Empire was known to possess the finest body of knowledge in the field of security psychology in the inhabited Galaxy."

"Hmm," said Keith-Ingram, frowning. "*Sarcasm*, do you think?"

Spangler hesitated. "I should like to be able to answer that with a definite no, but I can't be sure. Pembun is not an easy man to fathom."

"So I understand," said Keith-Ingram. "However, he has an absolutely impeccable record in the Outworld service. I don't think there can be any question of actual disloyalty."

Spangler was silent.

"Well, then," said Keith-Ingram testily, "what about this alleged pseudo-hypnotic ability of the Rithians? What does it amount to?"

"According to Pembun, complete control under very favorable conditions. He says, however, that the process is rather slow and limited in extent. In other words, that a Rithian might be able to take control of one or two persons if it could get them alone and unsuspecting, but that it would be unable to control a large group at any time or even a small group in an emergency.''

Keith-Ingram nodded. "Now, about this other matter of the protean ability—'' he glanced down at something on his own desk, outside the range of the scanner— "none of the available agents who have served in the Rithian system have anything even suggestive to report in that regard.''

Spangler nodded. "That could mean anything or nothing.''

"Yes,'' said the gray man. "On the whole, I'm inclined to feel as you evidently do, that there's nothing in it. Pembun may be competent and so on, but he's not Earth and he's not Security. Still, I don't have to remind you that if he's right on all counts, we've got a *very* serious situation on our hands.''

Spangler smiled grimly and nodded again. Keith-Ingram was noted for his barbed understatements. *If* Pembun was right, then it followed that the Empire's agents in the Rithian system had carried back no more information than the Rithians wanted them to have. . . .

Keith-Ingram rubbed his chin with a square, well-manicured hand. "Now, to date, the normal procedures haven't produced any result.''

"That's correct,'' Spangler admitted. Using all available personnel, it would take another four days to complete the house checks. Before that time, negative results would prove nothing.

"And according to Pembun, those procedures are no good. Now, has he proposed any alternate method, other than that beryllium-salts scheme of his?''

"No, sir. He held out no hope of results from that one under two and a half months.''

"Well, he may have something more useful to suggest. Ask him. If he does—try it.''

"Right,'' said Spangler.

"Good," said the gray man, giving Spangler his second-best smile. "Keep in touch, Thorne—and if anything else odd turns up, don't hesitate to call me direct."

The screen cleared.

Spangler stared at the vacant screen for a few moments, pursing his lips thoughtfully, then leaned back, absently fingering the banks of control studs at the edge of his desk.

Without any conscious warning, he found himself mentally reviewing the film taken in the Rithian system, which had been used in briefing Security personnel for the spy search.

First you saw only a riotous, bewildering display of green and gold; the shapes were so unfamiliar that the mind took several seconds to adjust. Then you perceived that the green was a swaying curtain of broad-leafed vines; the splashes of gold were intricate, many-petaled blossoms. Behind, barely noticeable, was a spidery framework of metal, and beyond that, an occasional glimpse of mist-blue that suggested open space.

Then the Rithian moved into view.

At first you thought "Spiders!" and Spangler remembered that he had jumped; spiders were a particular horror of his. Then, when the thing stopped in front of the camera, you saw that it was no more like a spider than like an octopus or a monkey.

Curiously, its outline most resembled those of the great golden blossoms. There was a circlet of tentacles, lying in gentle S-curves, and below that another. The thing's body was a soft sac that dangled beneath the lower set of tentacles; there was a head, consisting almost entirely of two huge, dull-red eyes. The creature's body was covered with short, soft-looking ochre fur or spines.

To some people, Spangler supposed, it would be beautiful—the sort of people who professed to find beauty in the striped, oval bodies of big beetles.

The thing turned quickly, hung still for another moment, and then clambered in a blur of limbs up the vine again.

Then there was another scene: darker green, this time—the gloom of a forest rather than a garden city. A Rithian moved into view, clinging to the slick purplish bole of a tree. Three of its fore-tentacles held a long, slender object that was obviously a weapon. It hung motionless for some minutes; then the gun moved slightly and a brilliant thread of violet flame lanced out from it. Far in the background something reddish shrieked and plummeted through the branches.

That was all, but that little was impressive enough. The weapon the film showed, evidently the equivalent of a light sporting rifle, compared favorably in performance with a Mark LV Becket.

There were other films: Spangler had not seen them, but he could imagine the kind of thing they must be. Pictures of Rithian factories, Rithian spaceships, Rithian laboratories. No matter what they were like in detail, in mass they had been impressive enough to convince Earth's strategists that making war on the Rithians might be disastrous.

So the slow campaign had begun: economic sabotage, subversion, propaganda. Nothing overt; nothing that could be surely traced to the Earthmen masquerading as non-Empire traders in the Rithian system. The tiny disruption bombs that had destroyed many another, weaker world would not be planted: the Rithians were a space-faring people, with colonies and a space fleet, and such a people can retaliate if their home world is destroyed. The campaign would be simply one of slow, patient attrition, designed to weaken the Rithians as a race and as a galactic nation; to divide them politically, hamper them economically and intellectually; to enmesh them in so subtle a net of difficulties that eventually, without knowing how it had come about, the Rithians would find that the crest of the wave had passed them by; that they were settling into the trough of history. It would take centuries. Earth could wait.

But the Rithians *had* discovered their enemies. And now the situation was grotesquely changed. No part of Earth's knowledge of the Rithians could any longer be considered reliable. The Rithians might be stronger or weaker than had been thought; the one thing that appeared certain was that they were not as they appeared in the films and the written reports that had reached Earth.

Even the best planning could not always succeed, Spangler thought. It was conceivable that Earth had finally met an antagonist against whom neither force nor subtlety would be of any use. Wonderingly, Spangler allowed his mind to focus on the idea of a universe in which the human race had been exterminated, like so many other races that had met superior force, superior subtlety. It was like trying to imagine the universe going forward after one's own death; intellectually, it was perfectly easy, emotionally, impossible.

At any rate, the game was not yet played out; and, Spangler reminded himself wryly, he was not charged with the responsibility of revising the Empire's military policy. He had one simple task to perform:

Find the Rithian.

Which brought him inevitably back to Pembun. Spangler's irritation returned, and grew. With a muttered, "*Damn* the man!" he stood and began pacing restlessly up and down his office.

Spangler was a career executive, not a Security operative; but he knew himself to be conscientious, thorough, interested in his work—and he had been in the Department for fifteen years. He ought not to feel about anyone as he felt about Pembun: baffled, uneasy, his mind filled with shadowy suspicions that had no source and no direction.

He had been through Pembun's dossier not once but three times: Ketih-Ingram was right, the man's record was absolutely clean. He was really what he seemed to be, a clumsy but devoted servant of the Empire. But—Spangler stopped. There was one thing which the dossier did not explain, and it was the first thing an agent of Security should want to know.

"What does he *want*?" Spangler asked aloud.

That was it—it located the sore spot that had been bothering Spangler for four days. What was Pembun after? What did he hope to accomplish? His talk was subtly flavored with amused contempt for the Empire and admiration for the Rithians. Then why was he working for one to defeat the other?

That was the thing to find out.

III

THE FLOW CHART OF ADMINISTRATION HILL WAS ENORmously complex. Processions of speedsters, coptercars and limousines merged, mingled and separated again; scooters, for intramural transport, moved in erratic lines among the larger vehicles and darted along the interoffice channels reserved for them alone. Traffic circles and cloverleaves directed and distributed the flow. At every instant, vehicles slipped out of the mainstream, discharged or loaded passengers, and were gone again. The cars, individually, were silent. In the aggregate, they produced a sound that just crossed the threshold of audibility—a single sustained tone that blended itself with the hum of a million conversations. The resulting sound was that of an enormous, idling dynamo.

Pembun's movements traced a thin, wavering line across all this confusion. And wherever he passed, he left a spreading wave of laughter in his wake.

At the intersection of Corridors Baker and One Zero, he tried to dismount from a scooter before it had come to a complete stop. The scooter's safety field caught him, half

on and half off, and held him, his limbs waving like an
angry beetle's until it was safe to put him down.

A ripple of laughter spread, and some of the recordists
and codex operators, with nothing better to do in their
morning break, followed him into the Section D commissary.

His experience with the scooter seemed to have dazed the
little man. He boarded the moving strip inside the commissary and then simply stood there, watching the room swing
past him. He made a complete circuit, passing a dozen
empty tables, and began another. The recordists and codex
girls nudged their friends and pointed him out.

On the third circuit, Pembun appeared to realize that he
would eventually have to get off. He put out a foot gingerly,
then drew it back. He faced in the other direction, decided
that was worse, and turned around again. Finally, with desperate resolution, he stepped off the slowly-moving strip.
His feet somehow got tangled. Pembun sat down with a
thud that shook the floor.

The laughter spread again. A man at a strip-side table got
something caught in his windpipe and had to have his back
pounded. Diners at more distant locations stood up to see
what was happening. Half a dozen people, trying to hide
their smiles, helped Pembun to his feet.

Pembun wandered out again. A blue-capped official guide
came forward, determinedly helpful, but Pembun, with ve-
hement gestures, explained that he was all right and knew
where he was going.

His bones ached, from his coccyx all the way up to his
cranium. That had been his sixth pratfall of the morning,
and there were others still to come.

He felt more than a little foolish—this place was so *big*!—
but he plowed through the press at the commissary entrance, signaled for another scooter and rode it half a
kilometer down the corridor.

On the walkway, just emerging from one of the offices,
was a group which included two people he knew: the darkly
mustachioed Colonel Cassina and his expressionless aide,
Captain Wei. Pembun waved happily and once more tried
to get off the scooter before it had stopped.

He writhed frantically in the tingling, unpleasant grip of the safety field. When it set him down at last, he charged forward, slipped, lost his balance, and—

The group wore a collective expression of joyful disbelief. There were suppressed gurglings, as of faulty plumbing; a nervous giggle or two from the feminine contingent; snickers from the rear. Colonel Cassina allowed himself a single snort of what passed with him for laughter. Even the impassive Captain Wei emitted a peculiar, high-pitched series of sounds which might be suggested by *"Tchee! tchee! tchee!"*

Helpful hands picked Pembun up and dusted him off. Cassina, his face stern again, said gruffly, "Don't get off before the thing stops, man. That way you won't get hurt." He turned away, then came back, evidently feeling the point needed more stress. *"Don't get off before the thing stops.* Understand?"

Pembun nodded, wordless. Mouth half open, he watched Cassina and Wei as they boarded a tandem scooter and swung off up Corridor Baker.

When he turned around, a disheveled Gordon was looming over him. "There you are!" cried the young man. "Really, Mr. Pembun, I've been looking for you upwards of an hour. Didn't you hear your annunciator buzzing?"

Pembun glanced at the instrument strapped to his right wrist. The movable cover was turned all the way to the left. "My!" he said. "I never thought about it, Mr. Gordon. Looks like I 'ad it turned off all the time."

Gordon smiled with his lips. "Well, I've found you, anyhow, sir. Can you come along to the Commissioner's office now? He's waiting to see you."

Without waiting for an answer, Gordon simultaneously hailed a double scooter and spoke into the instrument at his wrist.

"That's fine," said Pembun happily. "That was w'ere I 'ad a mind to go any'ow."

He boarded the scooter in front of Gordon, and this time followed Cassina's advice. He waited until the scooter had come to a complete stop, got off without difficulty, and strolled cheerfully into Spangler's office.

"Sorry I was 'ard to find," he said apologetically. "I 'ad my mind on w'at I was doing, and I didn' notice I 'ad my communicator turned of."

"Perfectly all right, Mr. Pembun," said Spangler, with iron patience. "Sit down. That's all, Gordon, thanks." He turned to Pembun. "Your suggestions are being followed up," he said curtly. "My immediate superior has directed me to ask you if you can help us still further by suggesting some new line of attack—one, for preferences, that won't require two or three months to operate."

"I was working on that," Pembun told him, "and not getting much of anyw'ere. But it doesn' matter now. I got another idea, and I was lucky. I found your Rithch."

As Spangler's face slowly froze, Pembun added, " 'E's Colonel Cassina's aide, Captain Wei."

Spangler began in a strangled voice, "Are you seriously saying—" He stopped, pressed a stud on the edge of his desk, and began again. "This conversation is being recorded, Mr. Pembun. You have just said that you have found the Rithian, and that he is Captain Wei. Tell me your reasons for that statement, please."

"Well, I better start at the beginning," said Pembun, "otherwise it won't make sense. You see, I 'ad a notion this Rithch might be a little worried. The fluoroscopes wouldn' bother 'im, of course, but the planet-wide embargo would. And so far as 'e knew, you might bring up something that would work better than fluoroscopes. So I thought it jus' might be possible that 'e'd 'ide 'imself in the middle of the people that were looking for 'im. That way, 'e'd be able to dodge your search squads, and 'e might stand a chance of getting 'imself out through the cordon. That was w'y 'e picked Colonel Cassina, seemingly. Any'ow, I thought it would strike 'im funny.

"So I went around making people lahf, jus' taking a chance. It was kind of 'ard, because like I told you, the Rithi got a primitive sense of yumor. Now, if you go and fall on your be'ind in front of a Rithch, 'e's going to lahf. 'E can't 'elp 'imself. That's w'at Captain Wei did. I've 'eard the Rithi lahf before. It sounds enough like yuman lahfter to fool you if you're not paying attention, but once you've 'eard it you'll never be mistaken. I'm telling you the truth, Commissioner. Captain Wei is the Rithch.''

Spangler, his lips thin, put his hand over the communicator plate. "Dossier on Captain Wei," he said.

"If you'll excuse me, Commissioner, I don' know w'ether 'e knows 'e gave 'imself away or not. If 'e knows we're after 'im and we don' catch 'im pretty quick, 'e's liable to do something we won't like.''

Spangler glanced at Pembun, his face sharp with irritation, and started to speak. Then his desk communicator buzzed and he put his hand over it. "Yes?"

Gordon's worried voice said, "There *is* no dossier on Captain Wei, Commander. I don't understand how it could have happened. Do you want me to check with District Archives in Denver?''

After a moment Spangler shot another glance at Pembun, a look compounded of excitement, intense dislike and unwilling respect. He said, "Do it later, Gordon. Meanwhile, get me Colonel Cassina, and then call the guardroom. I want all the available counter-Rithian trainees with full equipment, and I want them *now*.''

There was no doubt about it: "Captain Wei" was the Rithian spy. Somewhere, somehow, it must have managed to meet Cassina and make friends with him; or, at any rate, contrived to remain in his company long enough to take over control of Cassina's mind—to convince him, probably, that "Wei" was an old and valued friend, with whom Cassina had worked elsewhere; that "Wei" was now free to accept a new assignment, and that Cassina had already arranged for his transfer.

Introduced by Cassina, the supposed Chinese officer had passed without question. But there was no dossier in the files bearing that name. "Captain Wei" did not exist.

All this time, Spangler thought with a shudder, that monster had been living in their midst, sitting at their conferences, hearing everything that was planned against it. It must have been hard for it not to laugh.

The bitterest thing of all was that Pembun had found it. If it ever got out that a moon-faced colonial had solved

Spangler's problem for him by falling on his rear all over
Administration Hill . . .

Spangler impatiently put the thought out of his mind.
They were at the doorway to Cassina's private office. "Wei"
was in the smaller office immediately beyond; it commu-
nicated both with Cassina's suite and with the outer offices.

He saw the squad leader raise his watch to his ear. By
now the other half of the detail would have reached the outer
offices and quietly evacuated them. It must be time to go
in.

The squad leader opened the door, and Spangler stepped
in past him. Pembun was immediately behind; then came
the five operatives, all armed with immobilizing field projectors, and Mark XX "choppers"—energy weapons which,
in the hands of a skilled operator, would slice off an arm or
leg—or tentacle—as neatly as a surgeon could do it.

The operatives were encased from head to foot in tight,
seamless gasproofs. This, at any rate, was according to
standard operating procedure. The Rithian was urgently
wanted alive, but no chances could or would be taken.
"Weis' " room would be shut off by two planar force
screens, one projected by the standard equipment in Cassina's desk, the other by a portable projector set up by the
squad in the outer offices. At the same instant, the air-
conditioning ducts serving the room would be blocked off.
Inside the airtight compartment, the operatives would simultaneously gas and immobilize the Rithian; and if anything went wrong, they would use the choppers. It was a
maneuver that had been rehearsed by these men a hundred
times. Spangler was certain that nothing would go wrong.

Spangler had told Cassina nothing—had only asked if Wei
was in his office, then had hesitated as if changing his mind
and promised to call back in a few minutes. Now Cassina
stood up behind his desk, eyes bulging. "What's this?
What's this?" he said incredulously.

"Wei," Spangler said. "Stand out of the way, please,
Colonel. I'll explain in a moment."

"Explain!" said Cassina sharply. "See here, Spangler—"

The squad leader moved forward to the closed door of the inner office. At his signal, three of the remaining men took positions in front of the door; the other moved to herd Cassina out from behind his desk.

Cassina stepped aside, then moved suddenly and violently. Spangler, frozen with shock, saw him stiff-arm the approaching operative and instantly hurl himself into the group at the door. The group dissolved into a maelstrom of motion; then the door was open, Cassina had disappeared, and the others were untangling themselves and streaming in after him.

Spangler found himself running forward. A wisp of something acrid caught his throat; muffled shouts rang in his ears. A man's green-clad back blocked his view for an instant, then he darted to one side and could see.

The Rithian, his back oddly humped, was half-crouched over the dangling, limp body of Colonel Cassina. The monster's hands were clenched around Cassina's throat.

Everything was very clear, highly magnified.

A voice Spangler had not heard in years, the nasal, high-pitched voice of his Classics instructor, suddenly filled the room. Evidently the loudspeaker system had been turned on, though why they had got Professor Housty to declaim, *"The quality of mercy is not strained; it droppeth as the gentle rain . . ."* Spangler really could not say.

Everything had suddenly gone dead still, and the room was tilting very slowly to a vertiginous angle, while the tensed body of the Rithian—or was it really Captain Wei?—collapsed with equal slowness over the body of his victim. Spangler tried languidly to adjust himself to the tilting of the room, but he seemed to be paralyzed. There was no sensation in any part of his body. Then the floor got bigger and bigger, and at last turned into a dazzling mottled display that he watched for a long time before it grayed and turned dark.

"What happened?"

That was just the question Spangler wanted answered; he wished they had let him ask it himself. He tried to say something, but another voice cut in ahead of him.

"He went into the room without a suit. The gas got him."

Whom were they talking about? Slowly it dawned on Spangler that it was himself. That was it; that was why everything had been so strange a moment ago—

He opened his eyes. He was lying on the couch in his own private office. Two medical technicians, in pale-green smocks, were standing near the head of the couch. Farther down were Gordon, Miss Timoney, and the squad leader. Pembun was sitting in a chair against the wall.

One of the medics picked up Spangler's wrist and held it for a few seconds, then gently thumbed back one eyelid. "He's all right," he said, turning in Gordon's direction. "No danger at all." He moved away, and the other medic followed him out of the room.

Spangler sat up, swinging his legs over the side of the couch, and drew several deep breaths. He still felt a little dazed, but his head was clearing. He said to the leader, "Tell me what happened."

The leader had removed his gasproof and was standing bareheaded, in orange tights and high-topped shoes. He had an olive face, with heavy black brows and a stiff brush of graying black hair. He said, "You got a whiff of the gas, Commissioner."

"I know that, man," Spangler said irritably. "Tell me the rest."

"Colonel Cassina attacked us and forced his way into the inner office," the leader said. "We were taken by surprise, but we fired the gas jets and then got inside as fast as we could. When we got inside, we found the Rithian apparently trying to throttle Colonel Cassina. My men and I used the choppers, but, not to excuse ourselves, Commissioner, the Colonel interfered with our aim. The Rithian was killed."

Spangler felt an abrupt wave of nausea, and mastered it with an effort. "Colonel Cassina? How is he?"

"In bad shape, I understand, Commissioner."

"He's in surgery now, sir," Gordon put in. "He's alive, but his throat is crushed."

Spangler stood up a little shakily. "What's been done with the Rithian?"

"I've had the body taken down to the lab, sir," Gordon

said. "Dr. Baustian is there now. But they're waiting for your orders before they go ahead."

"All right," said Spangler, "let's get on with it."

He caught a glimpse of Pembun, with a curious expression on his face, trailing along behind the group as they left.

At first the corpse looked like the body of a young Chinese murdered by a meticulously careful ax-fiend: there was a gaping wound straight down from forehead to navel, then a perpendicular cross-cut, and then another gash down each leg.

Then they peeled the human mask away, and underneath lay the Rithian. The worst of it, Spangler thought, was the ochre fur: it was soft-looking, and a lighter color where it was rumpled—like the fur of the teddy bear he remembered from his childhood. But this was an obscene teddy bear, a thing of limp tentacles and dull bulging red eyes, with a squashy bladder at the bottom. It ought to have been stepped on, Spangler thought, and put into the garbage tube and forgotten.

It filled the human shell exactly. The top ring of tentacles had been divided, three on each side, to fit into "Wei's" arms. In the middle of each clump of tentacles, when the lab men pried them apart, was the white skeleton of a human arm; the shoulder joint emerged just under the ring. The tentacles in the second ring had been coiled neatly around the body, out of the way. The rest of the torso, and the leg spaces, had been filled by a monstrous bulging of the Rithian's sac-like abdomen.

Then the dissection started. . . .

Spangler stayed only because he could not think of a suitable excuse to leave; Cassina was still in shock and could not be seen.

Baustian and the other bio men were like children with new toys: first the muscles, and the nerve and blood and lymph systems in the "legs" the Rithian had formed from its shapeless body; then, when they cut open the torso, one bloody lump after another held up, and prodded, and exclaimed over. "Good Lord, look at this pancreas!" or "this liver!" or "this kidney!"

In the end, the resemblance to a teddy bear was nothing at all. The most horrible thing was that the more they cut, the more human the body looked. . . .

Later, he was standing in front of Cassina's door, and Pembun was holding his arm. "Don' tell 'im the Ritch is dead," the little man said urgently. "Tell 'im it was awl a mistake. Let 'im think w'at 'e likes of you. It may be important."

"Why?" Spangler asked vacantly.

Pembun looked at him with that same odd, haunted expression Spangler had noticed before, when they had left his office. He ought to be feeling cocky, Spangler thought vaguely, but he isn't.

" 'E's still in danger, Commissioner. 'E's not responsible for 'is own actions. You've got to convince 'im that you weren't after Wei at all, and that Wei's all right, otherwise I believe 'e'll try to kill 'imself."

"I don't understand you, Mr. Pembun," Spangler said. "How do you know the doctors or nurses haven't already told him?"

"I told them not to say anything," Pembun said, unabashed, "and let them think the order came from you."

Spangler's lips tightened. "We'll talk about this later," he said, and palmed the doorplate.

IV

CASSINA'S EYES WERE CLOSED. HIS FACE WAS A DEAD OLIVE-gray except for a slight flush on either cheekbone. He had the stupid, defenseless look of all sleeping invalids.

His head was supported by a hollow in the bolster; a rigid harness covered his neck. His mouth was slightly open under the coarse black mustachios, and a curved suction tube was hooked over his lower teeth.

The tube emitted a low, monotonous gurgling, which changed abruptly to a dry sucking noise. An attendant stepped forward and joggled the tube with one finger; the gurgling resumed.

As Spangler glanced away from the unconscious man, a medic came forward. He was tall and loose-limbed; his brown eyes gleamed with the brilliance that meant contact lenses. "Commissioner Spangler?"

Spangler nodded.

"I'm Dr. Householder, in charge of this section. You can question this man now, but I want you to avoid exciting him if you can, and don't stay longer than fifteen minutes after the injection. He's got half the pharmacopæia in him already."

Spangler stepped forward and sat down by the bedside.

At Householder's nod, a horse-faced female attendant set the muzzle of a pressure hypodermic against Cassina's bare forearm. She pressed the trigger, then unscrewed the magazine, dropped it into a tray and replaced it with another. In a moment Cassina sighed and opened his eyes.

Another attendant set a metal plate on the bed under Cassina's hand and gently forced a stylus between his fingers. Cables from plate and stylus led back around the foot of the bed to a squat, wheeled machine with a hooded screen. The attendant went to the machine, snapped a switch and then sat down beside it.

Cassina's eyes turned slowly until he discovered Spangler. He frowned, and seemed to be trying to speak. His lips moved minutely, but his jaw still hung open, with the suction tube hooked inside it. The monotonous gurgling of withdrawn sputum continued.

"Don't try to talk," Spangler said. "Your throat and jaw are immobilized. Use the stylus."

Cassina glanced downward, and his hand clenched around the slender metal cylinder. After a moment he wrote, "What have you done to Wei?"

The words crawled like black snakes across the white screen. Spangler nodded, and the attendant turned a knob; the writing vanished.

Spangler looked thoughtfully at Cassina. The question he had been expecting was, "What happened?"—meaning "What happened to me?" In the circumstances, the question was almost a certainty—probability point nine nine nine.

But Cassina had asked about Wei instead.

Grudgingly, Spangler said, "Nothing, Colonel. We weren't after Captain Wei, you know. The Rithian spy had concealed itself in his room. We couldn't warn Wei without alerting the Rithian."

Cassina stared gravely at Spangler, as if trying to decide whether he was lying. Spangler abruptly found himself gripping his knees painfully hard.

"He's all right?" Cassina scrawled.

"Perfectly," said Spangler. "Everything's all right. We've got the Rithian, and the alert is over."

Cassina drew a deep breath and let it out again. His mouth still hung idiotically slack, but his eyes smiled. He wrote, "What have you got me in this straitjacket for?"

"You were injured in the struggle. You'll be fit again in a few days. We're going to put you back to sleep now." Spangler motioned; the horse-faced girl put the hypo against Cassina's arm and pressed the trigger.

After a moment she said. "Colonel Cassina, we want you to write the numbers from one to fifty. Begin, please."

At "15" the scrawled numerals began to grow larger, less controlled; "23" was repeated twice, followed by a wild "17."

It was long after office hours, but Spangler still sat behind his desk. He had switched off the overhead illumination; the only light came from the reading screen in front of him. The screen showed a portion of the transcript of his interview with Cassina.

Spangler flipped over a switch and ran the film back to the beginning. He read the opening lines again.

> Q.: Can you hear me, Colonel?
> A.: Yes.
> Q.: I want you to answer these questions clearly, truthfully and fully to the best of your ability. When and where did you first meet Captain Wei?
> A.: In Daressalam, in October, 2501.
> Q.: Are you certain of that? Are you telling the truth?
> A.: Yes.

Cassina's conscious mind was convinced that he had first met "Wei" twenty years ago in the African District. Several repetitions of the question failed to produce any other answer. Spangler had tried to get around the obstacle by asking for the first meeting after December 18, 2521—the date of the Rithian agents' discovery by the city patrol.

He skipped a score of lines and read:

> Q.: What happened after that dinner?
> A.: I invited him up to my quarters. We sat and talked.

Q.: What was said?

A.: *(2 sec. pause)* I don't remember exactly.

Q.: You are ordered to remember. What did Wei tell you?

A.: *(3 sec. pause)* He told me—said he was Capt. Wei, served under me in the African District from 2501 to 2507. He—

Q.: But you knew that already, didn't you?

A.: Yes. No. *(2 sec. pause)* I don't remember.

Q.: I will rephrase the question. Did you or did you not know prior to that evening that Wei had served under you in the African District?

A.: *(3 sec. pause)* No.

Q.: What else did he tell you that night?

A.: Said he had done Naval Security work. Said he had applied for transfer, to be attached to me as my aide.

Q.: Did he tell you anything else, either instructions or information, other than details of your former acquaintance or details about his transfer, that evening?

A.: No.

Q.: Skip to your next meeting. What did he tell you on that occasion?

Gradually the whole story had come out, except one point. Spangler had struck a snag when he came to the evening of the 26th, two days ago.

Q.: What did Wei tell you that evening?

A.: *(4 sec. pause)* I don't remember. Nothing.

Q.: You are ordered to remember. What did he tell you?

A.: *(6 sec. pause: subject shows great agitation)* Nothing, I tell you.

Q.: You are ordered to answer, Colonel Cassina.

A.: *(subject does not reply; at the end of five seconds begins to weep)*

Dr. Householder: The fifteen minutes are up, Commissioner.

End trnscrpt 12.52 hrs. 12/22/2521

Later in the afternoon, after his first report to Keith-Ingram, Spangler had had another session with Cassina under the interrogation machine. He had drawn another blank, and had had to give up after five minutes because of Cassina's increasing distress. On being released from the machine, Cassina had gone into a coma and Householder declared that it would be dangerous to question him again until further notice.

Half an hour later, while he was talking to Pembun, Spangler had had a report that Cassina, still apparently unconscious, had made a strenuous effort to tear himself free of the protective collar and had gone into massive hemorrhage. He was now totally restrained, drugged, receiving continuous transfusion, and on the critical list.

Pembun. Pembun, Pembun. There was no escaping him: no matter where your thoughts led you, Pembun popped up at the end of the trail, as if you were Alice trying to get out of the Looking-Glass garden.

Pembun had been right again; Pembun was always right. They had triggered some post-hypnotic command in Cassina's mind, and Cassina, twitching to the tug of that string, had done his best to kill himself.

"It seems to me," Pembun had said that afternoon, "that the main question is—w'y did Colonel Cassina try so 'ard to get to the Rithch w'en 'e found out you were after 'im? 'E 'ad a command to do it, of course, but w'y? Not jus' to warn the Rithch, becawse 'e didn' get enough warning that way to do 'im any good, an' besides, if it was only that, w'y did the Rithch try to kill Cassina?"

"All right," Spangler had said, keeping his voice level with difficulty. "What's your explanation, Mr. Pembun?"

"Well, the Rithch mus' 'ave left some information buried in Cassina's subconscious that 'e didn' want us to find. I 'ad an idea that was it, and that's w'y I asked you not to tell Cassina the Rithch was dead—I thought 'e might 'ave been given another command, to commit suicide if the Rithch was discovered. I think we're lucky to 'ave Colonel Cassina alive today, Commissioner; I b'lieve 'e's the most important man in the Empire right now."

"That's a trifle strong," Spangler had said. "I won't deny

that this buried information, whatever it is, must be valu-
able. But what makes you assume that it's crucial? Presumably, it's a record of the Rithian's espionage or sabotage
activities . . .''

"Sabotage," Pembun had said quickly. "It coudn' be the
other, Commissioner, becawse the Ritch wouldn' care that
much if you found out something you already know. I b'lieve
Cassina knows this: 'e knows w'ere the bombs are buried.''

"Bombs!" Spangler had said after a moment. The idea
was absurd. "They wouldn't be so stupid, Mr. Pembun. We
have military installations on two hundred sixty planets, not
to mention the fleet in space. We'd retaliate, man. It would
be suicide for them to bomb us.''

"You don' understand, Commissioner. They don' want
to bomb Earth—if they did, there wouldn' 'ave been any
need for the Ritch to leave a record of w'ere the bombs
were. 'E'd simply set them with a time mechanism, and
that would be that. We couldn' do a thing till after they
went off. But 'e was the last one alive, an' 'e couldn' be
sure 'e'd get back with 'is information, so 'e 'ad to leave a
record. That only means one thing. The Rithi just want to
be able to warn us: *Leave us alone—or else.*' ''

Spangler's mind had worked furiously. It was terrifyingly
possible; he could find no flaw in it. Suitably placed, a few
score medium-sized disruption bombs would break a planet
apart like a rotten apple. "Medium-sized" meant approxi-
mately six cubic centimeters; they would be easy to smug-
gle, easy to conceal, almost impossible to find. The only
defense would be a radio-frequency screen over the whole
planet; and if the enemy knew the precise locations of the
bombs, even that defense would not work; a tight direc-
tional beam, accurately aimed, would get through and trigger the bombs. All it required was a race stubborn enough
to say, "Leave us alone—or else"—and mean it. From what
Pembun had said about the Rithians, they might well be
such a race.

But Earth played the percentages. Earth took only calculated risks. Earth would have to succumb.

That chain of reasoning had taken only a fraction of a

second. Spangler examined it, compared it with the known facts, and discarded it. He smiled.

"But, Mr. Pembun—*we've got* Cassina. It doesn't matter whether we get the information out of him or not; all we care about is that the *Rithians* aren't going to get it."

Pembun had looked absurdly mournful. "No, you're assuming that Cassina is the only one 'oo's got the information. I wish that was so, but I don' see 'ow it can be. Don' you see, giving it to Colonel Cassina was a mistake, becawse 'is mind is the obvious place for us to look. Now, I can see the Rithch making that mistake, deliberately, becawse it struck 'im so funny 'e couldn' resist it—but I can't see 'im making that mistake becawse 'e was stupid. I think Colonel Cassina was jus' an afterthought: 'e was feeling cocky, and 'e decided to plant the message one more time, right under your noses. I think 'e and 'is friends 'ad *already* planted it a 'undred or two 'undred times, 'owever many they 'ad time for. An' if it was me, I would 'ave picked interstellar travelers—agents for trading companies, executives who travel by spaceship a lot, visitors to Earth from other systems. I think that's w'at they did. If they did, it's practic'ly a mathematical certainty that their agents will eventually reach one of those people. You could keep up the embargo, not let anybody leave, but 'ow long would it take to process everybody 'oo might carry the message?"

"Years," Spangler had said curtly, staring at his desktop.

"That's right. It could be done, and if you were lucky it might work. But it would kill Earth just as sure as blowing it up. . . . We've got to find out what Colonel Cassina knows, Commissioner. There isn' any other way."

After that, the news about Cassina had come, almost as if it had been timed to underscore Pembun's words. Then the second and more painful interview with Keith-Ingram. Then Spangler had turned to some of the routine matters that had been filling his in-box all day, and quite suddenly it had been quitting time.

Spangler had started to leave, but had stopped at the door, turned to look at the silent, comforting walls, turned around and sat down at his desk again. Acting on an impulse he could hardly explain, he had called Joanna and begged off taking her to dinner. He had been sitting there, hardly moving, ever since.

He pressed the stud of his thumbwatch. "Eighteen eleven and twenty-five seconds."

Three hours: and he had had no dinner. There was a sickish taste in his mouth, and he felt a little light-headed, but not at all hungry.

He thumbed open the revolving front of the desk, took out a dispenser vial of pick-me-ups, and swallowed one moodily.

It came down to this, Spangler thought slowly. They had been very nearly beaten; except for one man—Pembun— they would have been beaten. And that was all wrong.

Pembun was uncouth, ill-educated, unmannered. His methods were the merest improvisation. He had intelligence, one was forced to admit, but it was crude, untutored and undirected. Yet he got results.

Why?

It was possible to explain all the events of the past two days simply by saying that Pembun had happened to possess special knowledge, not available to Security, which had happened to be just the knowledge needed. But that was an evasion. The knowledge was not "special"; it was knowledge Earth should have had, and had tried to get, and had failed to get.

Again, *why*?

It seemed to Spangler that since Pembun's arrival the universe had slowly, almost imperceptibly turned over until it was upside down. And yet nothing had changed. Pembun was the same; so were Spangler and the rest of the world he knew. It was a little like one of those optical illusions that you got in Primary Camouflage—a series of cubes that formed a flight of stairs going upward; and then you blinked, and the cubes were hollow, or the stairs were hanging upside down. Or like the other kind, the silhouettes of two men, with converging perspective lines at the top and bottom: you thought one man was much taller, but when you measured them you found that both were the same—or even that the one that had seemed smaller was larger than the other. . . .

Spangler swore. He had been on the point, he realized, of getting up, taking a scooter to G-level, Suite 111, and humbly asking Pembun to explain to him why the sun now revolved around the Earth, black was white, and great acorns from little oak trees grew.

He picked up a memocube and flung it violently onto the desk again.

The gesture gave him no relief; the feeling of rebellion passed; depression and bewilderment remained.

Like a moth to the flame—like Mohammed to the mountain—Spangler went to Pembun.

This time the door was closed.

After the space of three heartbeats, the scooter moved off silently down the way he had come, lights winking on ahead of it in the deserted corridor and fading when it passed. It turned the corner at Upsilon and disappeared, heading for the invisible lategoer who had signaled it.

Silence.

Down the corridor for five meters in either direction, glareless overhead lights showed Spangler every detail of the satin-finished walls, the mathematical lines of doors and maintenance entrances, the almost invisible foot-traces that, sometime during the night, would be vibrated into molecular dust and then gulped by suction tubes. Beyond was nothing but darkness. Far away, a tiny dot of light flared for an instant, like a shooting star, as someone crossed the corridor.

Spangler had an instant's vision of what it would be like if the whole thing were to stop: the miles of empty corridors, the darkness, the drifting dust, the slow invasion of insects. The dead weight of the Hill, bearing invisibly down upon you, the terrible, unsentient weight of a corpse.

Swallowing bile, he put his hand over the doorplate.

There was a long pause before the door slid open. Pembun, in underblouse and pantaloons, blinked at him as if he had been asleep. "Oh—Commissioner Spangler. Come awn in."

Spangler said hesitantly, "I'll talk with you tomorrow."

"No, please do come in, Commissioner. I'm glad you came. I was getting a little morbid, sitting 'ere by myself."

He closed the door behind Spangler. "Drink? I've still got 'alf the w'iskey left, and awl the soda."

The thought of a drink made Spangler's stomach crawl. He refused it and sat down.

On the table beside the recliner were several sheets of paper and an ornate old-fashioned electropen.

"I was jus' writing a letter to my wife," Pembun said, following his glance. "Or trying to." He smiled. "I can't tell 'er anything important without violating security, and I know I'll prob'ly get back to Ganymede before a letter would, after the embargo is lifted, any'ow, so there rilly wasn' much sense to it. It was jus' something to do."

Spangler nodded. "It's a pity we can't let you leave the Hill just now. But there's an amusement section right here, you know—cinemas, autochess, dream rooms, baths—"

Pembun shook his head, still smiling. "I wouldn' take any pleasure in those things, Commissioner."

His tone, it seemed to Spangler, was half regretful, half indulgent. No doubt they had other, more vigorous pleasures on Manhaven. Narcotics and mixed bathing would seem to them effete or incomprehensible.

Without knowing what he was about to say, he blurted, "Tell me truthfully, Pembun—do you despise us?"

Pembun's eyes widened slightly, then narrowed, and his whole face subtly congealed. "I try not to," he said quietly. "It's too easy. Did you come 'ere to ask me that, Commissioner?"

Spangler leaned forward, elbows on knees, clasping his hands together, "I think I did," he said. "Forgive my rudeness, Pembun, but I really want to know. What's wrong with us, in your view? What would you change, if you could?"

Pembun said carefully, "W'at would you say was your motive for asking that, Commissioner?"

Spangler glanced up. From this angle, Pembun looked somehow larger, more impressive. Spangler stared at him in a kind of rapture of discovery: the man's face was neither ugly nor ludicrous. The eyes were steady and alive with intelligence; the wide mouth was firm. Even the outsize ears, the heavy cheeks, only gave the face added strength and a curious dignity.

He said, "I want information. I've misjudged you grossly—and I apologize, but that's not enough. I feel that there must be something wrong with my basic assumptions, with the Empire. I want to know why we failed in the Rithian affair, and you succeeded. I think you can help me, if you will."

He waited.

Pembun said slowly, "Commissioner, I think you 'ave another motive, w'ether you rillize it consciously or not. Let me tell it to you, and see if you agree. Did you ever 'ear of pecking precedence in 'ens?"

"No," said Spangler. "By the way, call me Spangler, or Thorne, won't you?"

"All right—Thorne. You can cawl me Jawj, if you like. Now, about the 'ens. Say there are twelve in a yard. If you watch them, you'll find out that they 'ave a rigid social 'ierarchy. 'En A gets to peck all the others, 'en B pecks all the others but A, C pecks all but A and B, and so on down to 'en L, 'oo gets pecked by everybody and can't peck anybody back."

"Yes," said Spangler, "I see."

Pembun went on woodenly, "You're 'en B or C in the same kind of a system. There are one or two superiors that lord it over you and you do the same to the rest. Now, usually w'en anybody new comes into the yard, you know right away w'ether it's someone 'oo pecks you or gets pecked. But I'm a different case. I'm a different breed of 'en, and I don't rilly belong in your yard at all, so you try not to peck me excep' w'en I provoke you; it would lower your dignity. That's until you suddenly find that *I'm* pecking *you*. Now you've *got* to fit me into the system above yourself, becawse all this pecking wouldn' be endurable if you got it from both directions. So you came 'ere to say, 'I know you're 'igher in the scale than me, so it's all right. Go a'ead—peck me.' "

Spangler stared at him in silence. He was interested to observe that although he felt humiliated, the emotion was not actually unpleasant. It's a species of purge, he thought. It's good for us all to be taken down a peg now and then.

"What's more," Pembun said, watching him, "you enjoy it. It's a pleasure to you to kowtow to somebody you think is stronger, especially w'en your status and seniority aren't in any danger. Isn' that true?"

"I don't say you're wrong," Spangler answered, trying to be honest. "I've never heard it expressed just that way before, but it's certainly true that I'm conditioned to accept and exert authority—and you're quite right, I enjoy both acts. It's a necessary state of mind in my profession, or so I've always believed. I suppose it isn't very pretty, looked at objectively."

Pembun started to reach for the whiskey decanter, then drew his hand back. He looked at Spangler with a wry smile. "W'at you don' realize," he said, "is that I get no pleasure out of it. This may be 'ard for you to understand, but it's no fun for me to beat a man 'oos not trying to 'it me back. This 'ole conversation 'as been unpleasant to me, but I couldn' avoid it. You put me in a position w'ere no matter w'at I said, even if I rifused to talk to you at all, I'd be doing w'at you wanted. And this is the funny part, Commissioner—in making me 'urt your self-esteem, you've 'urt mine twice as bad. I expec' I'll 'ave a bad taste in my mouth for days."

Spangler stood up slowly. He took two deep breaths, but his sudden anger did not subside; it grew. He said carefully, "I don't need to have a mountain fall on me. That's a quaint expression we have, Mr. Pembun—it means that one clear and studied insult is enough."

Suddenly Pembun was just what he had seemed in the beginning: an irritating, dirty-faced, ugly beast of a *colonial*.

Pembun said, "You see, now you're angry. That's becawse I wouldn' play the pecking game with you."

Spangler said furiously, "Mr. Pembun, I didn't come here for insults, or for barnyard psychology either. I came to ask you for information. If you are so far lost to common civility—" The sentence slipped out of his grasp; he started again: "Perhaps I had better remind you that I'm empowered to *demand* your help as an official of the Empire."

Pembun said, unruffled, "I'm 'ere to 'elp if I can, Commissioner. W'at was it you wanted, exactly?"

"I asked you," said Spangler, "to tell me what, in your opinion, were the causes of Security and War Department failure in the Rithian case." As Pembun started to speak, he cut in: "Put your remarks on a spool, and have it on my desk in the morning." His voice sounded unnaturally loud in his own ears; it occurred to him with a shock that he had been shouting.

Pembun shook his head sadly, reprovingly. "I'll be glad to—if you put your request in writing, Commissioner."

Spangler clenched his jaw. "You'll get it tomorrow," he said. He turned, opened the door and strode away down the empty corridor. He did not stop to signal for a scooter until he had turned the corner, and Pembun's doorway was out of sight.

He found Joanna in the tower room, lying against a section of the couch that was elevated to form a backrest. The room was filled, choked to bursting by a male voice shouting incomprehensible syllables against a strident orchestral background. Spangler's brain struggled futilely with the words for an instant, then rejected them in disgust. The recording was one of Joanna's period collection, sung in one of the dead languages. German; full of long vowels and fruity sibilants.

She waved her hand over the control box, and the volume diminished to a bearable level. She stood up and came to meet him.

"I thought you sounded upset when you called," she said, and kissed him. "Sit here. Put your feet up. Have you had anything to eat?"

"No," said Spangler. "I couldn't; I'm too tired for food."

"I'll have something up. You needn't eat it if you don't want to."

"Fine," he said with an effort.

She dialed the antique food-selector at the side of the couch, then came to sit beside him.

The voice was still shouting, but as if it were a long

distance off. It rose to a crescendo, there was a dying gasp
from the orchestra, a moment's pause, and then another
song began.

"Why don't you have that translated?" he asked irritably.

"I don't know; I rather like it as it is. Shall I turn it off?"

"That's not the point," said Spangler with controlled
impatience. "You like it as it is—why? Because it's incomprehensible? Is that a sane reason?"

The food-selector's light glowed. Joanna opened the hop-
per, took out a tube of broth and a sandwich loaf, and put
them on the table at Spangler's elbow.

"What are you really angry about, Thorne?" she asked
quietly.

"I'll tell you," said Spangler, sitting erect. The words
spilled out of him, beyond his control. "Do you think it
isn't obvious to me, and to everyone else who knows you,
what you're doing to yourself with this morbid obsession?
Do you think it's pleasant for me to sit here and watch you
wallowing in the past, like a dog in carrion, because you're
afraid of anything that hasn't been safely buried for five
hundred years?"

Her eyes widened with shock, and Spangler felt an answering wave of pure joy. This was what he had come here
to do, he realized, though he hadn't known it before. It was
what he should have done long ago. She blushed furiously
from forehead to breast, then turned ivory-pale.

"Stop it," she said in a tight voice.

"I won't stop," Spangler said, biting the words. "Look
at yourself. You're half-alive, half a woman. You let just
enough of yourself live to do your work, and answer when
you're spoken to, and respond to your lover. The rest is
dead and covered with dust. I can taste it when I kiss you.
How do you think I feel, wanting you, knowing that you're
out of my reach—not because . . ."

She got up and started toward the door. Spangler reached
her in one stride, pushed her backward onto the couch and
held her there with his whole weight.

". . . not because you belong to anyone else, or ever
will, but because you're too timid, too selfish, too wrapped
up in yourself ever to belong to anybody?"

She struggled ineffectively. Her eyes were unfocused and glazed with tears; her whole body was trembling.

Spangler tore open her gown, pulled it away from her body. "Go ahead, look at yourself! You're a woman, a living human being, not a mummy. Why is that so hateful? Do you get any pleasure from killing yourself and everything you touch?" He shook her. "Answer me!"

She gasped, "I can't . . ."

"What can't you? You can feel, you can speak, you can do anything a normal human being can do, but you won't. You wouldn't leave that smug little shell of yours to save a life. You wouldn't leave it to save the Empire—not even to save yourself."

"Let me go."

"You're not sick, you're not afraid, you're just selfish. Cold and selfish. Everything for Joanna, and let the rest of the universe go hang!"

"Let me go."

Her trembling had stopped; she was still breathing hard, but her pale lips were firm. She raised her lids and looked at him squarely, without blinking.

Spangler raised his open right hand and struck her in the face. Her head bobbed. She looked at him incredulously, and her mouth opened.

Spangler hit her again. At the third blow, the tears started again. Her face crumpled suddenly and a series of short, animal sounds came out of her. At the fourth, she stopped trying to turn her head aside. Her body was limp, her eyes closed and without expression. Her sobs were as mechanical and meaningless as a fit of the hiccoughs.

Spangler rolled away from her, stood up and went to the chair. He felt purged and empty. There was a heavy tiredness in his limbs; he could feel his heart beating slowly and strongly. He said tonelessly, "You can get up now. I won't hit you again."

After a moment she sat up, spine curved, head hanging. When she got to her feet and turned toward the bathroom door, Spangler followed and stepped in front of her, grasping her arms.

"Listen to me," he said. "You're going to marry me, and we're going to be happy. Do you understand that?"

She looked at him without interest.

"You fool," she said.

She stood motionless until he let her go, and then moved without haste through the doorway. The door closed behind her, and Spangler heard the lock click.

V

SPANGLER ENTERED HIS OFFICE, AS HE USUALLY DID, HALF an hour before the official opening time. He had sat up for a long time after leaving Joanna's tower the night before, and had slept badly afterward. This morning he had a headache which the pick-me-ups would not entirely suppress; but his mind felt cold and clear. He knew precisely what he wanted to do.

Last night's blunder was not irreparable. It was all but disastrous; it was criminally foolish; it had set him back at least six months; but it had not beaten him.

His first move would be to send her a present: something she would prize too much to reject—old paintings, or books or recordings. Very likely there would be something of the sort among the property seized by the Department in treason cases; if not, he would get it from a private collector. He had already composed the note to go with the gift: it was humble without servility, regretful without hope. It implied that he would not see her again; and he would not—not for at least a month.

The last three weeks of that time Spangler had allotted to grand strategy—planting rumors, sure to reach Joanna: that he was overworking; that he never smiled; that he was ill but had refused treatment. That sort of thing, details to be worked out later.

The first week was dedicated to an altogether different purpose. His ruinous outburst last night had at least had one good effect; it had taught Spangler that he could not fight both battles at once. Commencing today, his total energies would be aimed at one objective: to crush Pembun.

It could be done; it would be done. He had underestimated the man, but that was over. From now on, things would be different.

"Ten hours," said his thumbwatch.

On his desk was a spool of summarized reports addressed to him from Keith-Ingram. The activities of the Rithians had now been partly traced: eight of them, traveling together, had reached Earth as passengers aboard a second-rate tramp freighter, docking at Stambul, on the evening of December 10th. From Stambul they were known to have taken the stratosphere express to Paris, but no further trace of their movements had so far turned up until seven of them appeared in Albuquerque on the 18th, with one exception: the eighth Rithian had shipped out aboard a liner leaving for the Capri system on the 12th, only two days after the group had arrived. It had disembarked at Lumi, where its trail ended.

Doubtless, Spangler thought, it had changed its disguise there and continued by a devious route. By now it was back in the Rithian system.

Its return before the others' was puzzling. Obviously the group had not finished its collective task, or the others would have got out too; either it had had a separate assignment, which it had completed before the others, or some single item of information had been turned up which the Rithians thought sufficiently important to send a messenger back with it immediately.

He glanced quickly through the conference schedule which Miss Timoney had made up the previous afternoon, then laid it aside and spent the rest of his half-hour in dictating notes to Pembun, Keith-Ingram and Dr. Baustian.

The note to Pembun repeated yesterday's question, word for word.

Keith-Ingram's reported the condition of Colonel Cassina and gave Pembun's analysis of the situation, without comment.

Baustian's requested him to submit, as soon as possible, a reliable procedure for identifying Rithians masquerading as human beings.

Pembun's reply popped into his in-box almost immediately; the man must have prepared it last night and held it ready for Spangler's formal request.

Spangler put the spool viciously into the screen slot and skimmed through it. It was in reasonably good Standard; so good, in fact, that Spangler conceived an instant suspicion that Pembun could speak Standard acceptably when he chose.

The document read, in part:

In my judgment, the most serious weakness of Empire executive personnel is an excessive reliance on prescribed methods and regulations, and inadequate emphasis on original thinking and personal initiative. I am aware that this is in accord with overall policy, which would be difficult if not impossible to alter completely within the framework of the Empire, but it is my feeling that attention should be given to this problem at high policy levels, and efforts made to alter existing conditions if possible.

It is not within my competence to suggest a model of procedure, especially since the problem appears to be partly philosophical in nature. The tendency of Empire executive personnel to interpret regulations and directives in a rigid and literal manner is in my opinion clearly related to the increasing tendency toward standardization in Home World art, manners, customs and language. In the final category, I would cite the obsolescence of all Earth languages except Standard, and in Standard, the gradual elimination of homonyms and synonyms, as well as the increasing tendency to restrict words to a single meaning, as especially significant. . . .

Spangler removed the spool and tossed it into his "awaiting action" box. A moment later it was time for his first conference.

He had left word with Gordon to give him any message from Baustian as soon as it arrived. Forty-five minutes after the conference began, a spool popped into the in-box in front of him.

Colonel Leclerc, Cassina's replacement, had been giving a long and enthusiastic account of certain difficulties encountered by the Fleet in maintaining the supra-Earth cordon, and the means by which they were being overcome. Leclerc was the oldest man at the table, and fairly typical of the holdovers from the last generation but one, when, owing to the shortage of governmental and miltary personnel caused by the almost-distastrous Cartagellan war, standards had been regrettably lax. He was the sort of man one automatically thought of as "not quite class." His manner was a little too exuberant, his gestures too wide, his talk imprecise and larded with anachronisms.

Spangler waited patiently until he paused to shrug, then cut in smoothly: "Thank you, Colonel. Now, before we continue, will you all pardon me a moment, please?"

He slipped the spool into place and lighted the reading screen. The note read:

Baustian, G. B., BuAlPhyl
Spangler, T., DeptSecur
MS MU
12/29/2521
BAP CD18053990
Ref DS CD50347251

1. Recommended procedure for identifying members of the Rithian race masquerading as humans is as follows:
2. Make 1.7 cm. vertical incision, using instrument coated with paste of attached composition (Schedule A), in mid-thigh or shoulder region of subject. Rea-

gent, in combination with Rithian body fluids, will produce brilliant purple precipitate. No reaction will take place in contact with human flesh.

3. For convenience of use, it is recommended that incision be made by agency of field-powered blade in standard grip casing, as in attached sketches. (Schedule B)

4. If desired, blade coating may also contain soporific believed to be effective in Rithian body chemistry. (Schedule C)

5. End.

Att   BAP CD18053990A
       BAP CD18053990B
       BAP CD18053990C

Spangler smiled and cleared the screen.

"The information is satisfactory, Commissioner?" asked Colonel Leclerc.

"Quite satisfactory, Colonel." Quickly, so as to give Leclerc no opportunity to launch himself into his subject again, Spangler turned to Pemberton, the mayor's aide. "Mr. Pemberton?"

The young man began querulously, "We don't want to seem impatient, Commissioner, but you know that our office is under considerable strain. Now, you've given us to understand that the Rithian has already been captured and killed, and what we want to know is, how much longer . . ."

Spangler heard him out as patiently, to all outward appearance, as if he had not heard the same complaint daily since the embargo began. He put Pemberton off smoothly but noncommittally, and adjourned the conference.

Back in his office, Spangler finished reading Baustian's note and dictated an endorsement of paragraphs one to three. Paragraph four was a good notion, but anything with a rider like that on it would take twice as long to go through channels.

Spangler rewound the spool and set the machine to make three copies, one of which he addressed to Keith-Ingram, one to Baustian, and the third to the man in charge of the fabricators assigned to Security, with an AAA priority. Then he took out Pembun's message and read it through carefully.

> With regard to the assumed success of the Rithian pseudo-hypnosis against Empire agents, I would again suggest that the basic fault may be deeply rooted in the social complex of Earth, and in the rigid organization of Empire administration. On most of the Outworlds of the writer's experience, good hypnotic subjects are in a minority, but my impression is that this is not the case on Earth, at least among Empire personnel. It may be said that a man who has successfully absorbed all the unspoken assumptions and conditioned attitudes required of him by responsible position in the Empire is already half hynotized; or to put it differently, that non-suggestible minds tend to be weeded out by the systems of selection and promotion in use. For example, the addressee, Commissioner T. Spangler, is in the writer's opinion suggestible in the extreme. . . .

Spangler grinned angrily and rewound the spool.

How typical of the man that report was!—a solid gelatinous mass of naïveté surrounding one tiny thorn of shrewdness. In Pembun's place, Spangler would simply have disclaimed ability to answer the question. Since Pembun was not employed by any department concerned, the reply would have been plausible and correct; nothing more could ever have come of it.

That must have occurred to Pembun; and yet he had gone stolidly ahead to answer the question fully, and, Spangler was ready to believe, honestly. It was a damaging document; some phrases in it, particularly "within the framework of the Empire," were clearly treasonable. But he had written it; and then he had slipped in that comment about Spangler.

That comment was just damaging enough to Spangler to offset the mildly damaging admissions Pembun had made about himself. Therefore Pembun had actually taken no risk at all. But why had he troubled to dictate a carefully-phrased quarter-spool to be buried in the files, when a disclaimer, in two lines, would have served? Just for "something to do?"

Spangler thought not. There was a curious coherence in Pembun's oddities: they all hung together somehow. Wincing, he forced himself to go back over the recollection of last night. There again, from the normal point of view, Pembun had given himself unnecessary difficulty. Confronted with that inconvenient question of Spangler's, "What's wrong with the Empire?" and the even more embarrassing, "Do you despise us?" any ordinary person would simply have lied.

At any rate, Pembun, by his own statement, had got no pleasure from telling the truth. What was that remark? ". . . a bad taste . . ." Never mind. What emerged from all this, Spangler thought, was the picture of a man who was compulsively, almost pathologically honest. Yes, that expressed it. His frankness was not even ethico-religious in character: it was symbolic, a *gesture*.

Spangler felt himself flushing, and his lips tightened.

The question remained: What did the man want?

He had no answer yet; but he had a feeling that he was getting closer.

At eleven hours a report came from the head of the infirmary's psychiatric section. The information Security wanted from Colonel Cassina was still unavailable and in PsytSec's opinion could not be forced from him without a high probability of destroying the subject's personality. Did Spangler have the necessary priority to list Colonel Cassina as expendable?

At eleven-ten, a call came through from Keith-Ingram.

"On this Cassina affair, Thorne, what progress are you making?"

Spangler told him.

Keith-Ingram rubbed his square chin thoughtfully. "That's unfortunate," he said. "If you want my view, the Empire can spare Colonel Cassina, all right, but I'll have to go to the High Assembly for permission, and the Navy

will fight it, naturally. I rather wish there were another way.
Have you consulted Pembun about this?''

"The report had just come in when you called.''

"Well, let's get this cleaned up now, if we can. Get him
on a three-way, will you?''

Face stony, Spangler made the necessary connections.
The image of Keith-Ingram dwindled and moved over to
occupy one half of the screen. In the other half, Pembun
appeared.

Keith-Ingram said, "Now, Mr. Pembun, you've helped
us out of the stew right along through this affair. Have you
any suggestions that might be useful in this phase of it?''

Pembun's expression was blandly attentive. He said,
"My, that would be a 'ard decision to make. Let me think
a minute.''

Out of screen range, Spangler's fingers moved spasmod-
ically over the edge of his desk.

Finally Pembun looked up. "I got one notion,'' he said.
"It's kind of a long chance, but if it works it will get you
the information you want without 'urting the Colonel. I was
thinking that w'en the Rithi planted that information, they
mus' 'ave given their subject some kind of a trigger stimulus
to unlock the message. Now, if the trigger is verbal, we
'aven' got a chance of 'itting it by accident. But it jus' now
struck me that the trigger might be a situation instead of a
phrase or a sentence. I mean, it might be a combination of
diff'rent kinds of stimuli—a certain smell, say, plus a certain color of the light, plus a certain temperature range, and
so on.''

"That doesn't sound a great deal more hopeful, Mr.
Pembun,'' Spangler put in.

"Wait,'' said Keith-Ingram, "I think I see what he's getting at. You mean, don't you, Mr. Pembun, that the Rithians
might have used as a stimulus complex the normal conditions on their home world?''

"That's it,'' Pembun told him with a smile. "We can't
be sure they did, of cawse, but it seems to me there's a fair
chance. Any'ow, it isn' as far-fetched as it sounds, becawse
those conditions would be available to the Rithi on any
planet w'ere any number of them live. You wawk into a

Rithch's 'ouse, an' you think you're on Sirach. They're use' to living in those vine cities of theirs, you see. They 'ate to be penned up. So w'en they 'ave to live in 'ouses, they put up vines in front of illusion screens, an' use artificial light an' scents, an' fool themselves that way.''

"I see," said Keith-Ingram. "That sounds very good, Mr. Pembun; the only question that occurs to me is, can we duplicate those conditions accurately?''

"I should think so," Pembun answered. "It shouldn' be too 'ard.''

"Well, I think we'll give it a trial, at any rate. What do you say, Thorne? Do you agree?''

Spangler could tell by the almost imperceptible arch of Keith-Ingram's right eyebrow, and the frozen expression of his mouth, that he knew Spangler didn't and was enjoying the knowledge.

"Yes, by all means," said Spangler politely.

"That's settled then. I'll leave you and Thorne to work out the details. Clearing.'' His image faded out, leaving half the screen blank.

Spangler said coldly, "This is your project, Mr. Pembun, and I'll leave you entirely in charge of it. Requisition any space, materials and labor you need, and have the heads of sections call me for confirmation. I'll want reports twice daily. Are there any questions?''

"No questions, Commissioner.''

"Clearing.''

Spangler broke the connection, then dialed Keith-Ingram's number again. He got the "busy" response, as he expected, but left the circuit keyed in. Twenty minutes later Keith-Ingram's face appeared on the screen. "Yes, Spangler? What is it now? I'm rather busy.''

Spangler said impassively, "There are two matters I wanted to discuss with you, Chief, and I thought it best not to bring them up while Pembun was on the circuit.''

"Are they urgent?''

"Quite urgent.''

"All right then, what are they?''

"First," said Spangler, "I've sent you a note on a new

testing method of Baustian's, for detecting any future Rithian masqueraders. I'd like to ask you for permission to
use it here in the Hill, in advance of final approval, on a
provisional test basis."

"Why?"

"Just a precaution, sir. We've found one Rithian here; I
want to be perfectly sure there aren't any more."

Keith-Ingram nodded. "No harm in being sure. All right,
Thorne, go ahead if you like. Now what else was there?"

"Just one thing more. I'm wondering if it wouldn't be a
sound idea to open the question of Cassina's expendability
anyhow, regardless of this scheme of Pembun's. If it turns
out to be a frost, there'll be less delay before we can go
ahead with the orthodox procedure." His stress on the word
"orthodox" was delicate, but he knew Keith-Ingram had
caught it.

The older man gazed silently at him for a moment. "As
a matter of fact," he said, "it happens that I'd already
thought of that. However, I may as well say that I have
every confidence in Pembun. If all our personnel were as
efficient as he is, Thorne, things would go a great deal more
smoothly in this department."

Spangler said nothing.

"That's all then? Right. Clearing."

Recalling that conversation before he went to bed that
night, Spangler thought, We'll see how much confidence
you have in Pembun this time tomorrow.

Everything was ready by ten hours.

There was no puzzle, Spangler thought with satisfaction,
without a solution. No matter how hopelessly involved and
contradictory a situation might appear on the surface, or
even some distance beneath it, if you kept on relentlessly,
you would eventually arrive at the core, the quiet place
where the elements of the problem lay exposed in their basic
simplicity.

And this was the revelation that had been vouchsafed to
Spangler:

The real struggle was between savagery and civilization,

between magic and science, between the double meaning and the single meaning.

Pembun was on the side of ambiguity and lawlessness. Therefore he was an enemy.

What had blinded Spangler, blinded them all, was the self-evident fact that Pembun was *human*. Loyalty to a nation or an idea is conditioned; but loyalty to the race is bred in the bone. As the old saying had it, "Blood is thicker than ichor."

Pembun's humanity was self-evident; but was it a fact?

"Wei" had been a human being, too—until the moment when he was unmasked as a monster.

Pembun belonged to a world so slovenly that Rithians were allowed to come and go as they pleased. Was it not more than possible, was it not almost a tactical certainty, that given opportunity and the made-to-order usefulness of Pembun's connection with the Empire, they had at the least made him their agent?

Or, at most, replaced him with one of themselves?

The idea was fantastic, certainly. The picture of Pembun playing the role of Rithian-killer, deliberately betraying his confederate in order to safeguard his own position, was straight out of one of those wild twentieth-century romances—the kind in which the detective turned out to be the murderer, the head of the Secret Police was also the leader of the Underground, and, as often as not, the subordinate hero was a beautiful girl disguised as a boy by the clever stratagem of cutting her hair.

But that was precisely the kind of world that Pembun came from, whether he was human or Rithian: that was the unchanging essence of the ancient Unreason, beaten now on Earth but not yet stamped out of the cosmos. That was the enemy.

"Ten oh-one," said his watch. In a few moments, now, one part of the question would be answered.

He glanced at the four men in workmen's coveralls who stood by an opened section of the wall. One of them held what appeared to be a cable cutter; the others had objects that looked like testing instruments and spare-part kits. The

"cutter," underneath its camouflage shell, was an immobilizing field projector; the rest were energy weapons.

The men stood quietly, not talking, until a signal light
flashed on Spangler's desk. He nodded, and they crouched
nearer to the disemboweled wall, beginning a low-voiced
conversation. A moment later, Pembun appeared in the
doorway.

Spangler glanced up from his reading screen, frowning.
"Oh, yes—Pembun," he said. "Sit down a moment, will
you?" He gestured to one of the chairs along the far wall.
Pembun sat, hands crossed in his lap, idly watching the
workmen.

Spangler thumbed open the front of his desk and touched
a stud; a meter needle swung far over and held steady. The
room was now split into two parts by a planar screen just
in front of the desk. Spangler closed the microphone circuit
which would carry his voice around the barrier.

The intercom glowed; Spangler put his hand over it.
"Yes?"

The man said, as he had been instructed, "Commissioner, is Mr. Pembun in your office?"

"Yes, he is. Why?"

"It's that routine test, sir. You told us to give it to everybody who'd been in the Hill less than six months, and Mr.
Pembun is on our list. If you're not too busy now—"

"Of course—he would be on the list," Spangler said.
"That hadn't occurred to me. All right, come in." He
turned to Pembun. "You don't mind?"

"What is it?" Pembun asked.

"We have a new anti-Rithian test," Spangler said easily.
"We're just making absolutely certain there aren't any more
Weis in the Hill. In your case, of course, it's only a for-
mality."

Pembun's expression was hard to read, but Spangler
thought he saw a trace of uneasiness there. He watched
narrowly as a white-smocked young man carrying a medical
kit came in through the door to Pembun's right.

The workmen separated suddenly, and two of them started
toward the door. When they had taken a few steps, one of

them turned to call back to the remaining two. "You certain two RBX's will do it?"

"What's the matter, don't you think so?"

"It's up to you, but . . ." The men went on talking, while the medic approached Pembun and opened his kit. "Mr. Pembun?"

"Yes."

"Will you stand up and turn back your right sleeve, please?"

Pembun did as he was told. His upper arm was shapeless with overlaid fat and muscle, like a wrestler's. The medic placed one end of a chromed cylinder against the fleshy part of the shoulder, and pressed the release. Pembun started violently and clapped his hand to the injury. When he took it away, there was a tiny spot of blood on his palm.

The medic extruded the cylinder's narrow blade and showed it to Spangler. "Negative, Commissioner."

"Naturally," Spangler said dryly. The medic tore off a swab from his kit and wiped Pembun's wound, then put a tiny patch of bandage on it, closed his kit and went away.

Negative, Spangler thought regretfully. Too bad; it would have been gratifying to find out that Pembun had tentacles under that blubber. But it had been a pleasure to watch him jump, anyhow. He opened his desk and cut the field circuit.

The two workmen near the door finished their discussion and left. Spangler said to the remaining pair, "Will you wait outside for a few minutes, please?"

When they had gone, Pembun came forward and took the seat facing the desk. "That's a rough test," he said. " 'Ow does it work?"

Spangler explained. "Sorry if it was unpleasant," he added, "but I believe it's more effective than the old one."

"Well, I'm glad I passed, any'ow," said Pembun, poker-faced.

"To be sure," said Spangler. "Now—your report, Mr. Pembun?"

"Well, I've 'ad a little trouble. I asked Colonel Leclerc to see if 'e couldn' send somebody to Santos in the Shahpur system, to get some Rithi city-vines from the botanical garden there. 'E gave me to understand that you rifused the request."

"Yes, I'm sorry about that," Spangler said. "Until this question is settled, we can't very well relax the embargo, especially not for an Outworld jump."

Pembun accepted that without comment. "Another thing that 'appened, I wanted copies of any Rithi films the War Department might 'ave, in 'opes that one of them would include a sequence of a Rithch I could use to build up the illusion there was a Rithch in the room. That was rifused too; I don't know w'ether it went through your office or not."

"No, this is the first I've heard of it," Spangler lied blandly, "but I'm not surprised. War is extremely touchy about its M. S. files—I'm afraid you'd better give up hope of any help there. Can't you make do without those two items?"

Pembun nodded. "I figured I might 'ave to, so I went a'ead and did the best I could. I don't promise it will work, becawse some of it is awful makeshift, but it's ready."

Spangler felt a muscle jump in his cheek. "It's ready *now*?" he demanded.

"W'enever you like, Commissioner." Pembun got up and turned toward the door.

Spangler made an instant decision. He had not planned to take the second step against Pembun until he had manufactured a plausible opportunity, but he couldn't let Pembun's examination of Cassina proceed. He said sharply, "Just a moment!" and added, "If you don't mind."

As Pembun paused, he put out his hand to the intercom. "Ask those workmen to step in here again, will you?"

The door opened, and all four of the pseudo-workmen trooped in. Pembun looked at them with an expression of mild surprise. " 'Aven' you got those RBX's *yet*?" he asked.

No one answered him. Spangler said, "I'll trouble you to come down to the interrogation rooms with me, Mr. Pembun." At his gesture, the four men moved into position around Pembun, one on either side, two behind.

"Interrogation!" said Pembun. "W'y, Commissioner?"

"Not torture, I assure you," Spangler replied, coming around the desk. "Just interrogation. There are a few questions I want to ask you.''

''Commissioner Spangler,'' said Pembun, ''am I to understand that I'm suspected of a crime?''

''Mr. Pembun,'' Spangler answered, ''please don't be childish. Security is empowered to question anyone, anywhere, at any time, and for any reason.''

VI

AFTER THE INITIAL STRUGGLE, PEMBUN HAD RELAXED. HE was breathing shallowly now, his eyes half open and unfocused.

"Have you got enough test patterns?" Spangler asked, using a finger-code.

"Yes, I think so, Commissioner," the young technician replied in the same manner. "His basics are very unusual, though. I may have some trouble interpreting when we get into second-orders."

"Do the best you can." He leaned forward, close to Pembun's head. "Can you still hear me, Pembun?" he said aloud.

"Yes."

"State your full name."

"Jawj Pero Pembun."

"How long have you been an agent of the Rithians?"

A pause. "I never was."

Spangler glanced at the technician, who signaled, "Emotional index about point six."

Spangler tried again. "When and where did you last meet a Rithian before coming to Earth?"

"In April, twenty-five fourteen, at the Spring Art Show in Espar, Man'aven."

"Describe that meeting in detail."

"I was standing in the crowd, looking at a big canvas called 'Yeastley and the Tucker.' The Rithch came up and stood beside me. 'E pointed to the painting and said, 'Very amusing.' 'E was looking at the picture through a transformer, so the colors would make sense to 'im. I said, 'I've seen Rithi collages that looked funnier to me.' Then 'e showed me 'ow, by changing the transformer settings, you could make it look like Yeastley 'ad a mouldy face with warts on it, and the Tucker 'ad a long tail. I said . . .''

Pembun went on stolidly to the end of the incident; he and the Rithch, whose name he had never learned, had exchanged a few more remarks and then parted.

The emotional index of his statement did not rise above point nine on a scale of five.

"Before that, when and where was your last meeting with a Rithch?"

"On the street in Espar, early in December, twenty-five thirteen."

"Describe it."

Spangler went grimly on, taking Pembun farther and farther back through innumerable casual meetings. At the end of half an hour, Pembun's breathing was uneven and his forehead was splotched with perspiration. The technician gave him a second injection. Spangler resumed the questioning.

Finally:

". . . Describe the last meeting before that."

"There was none."

Spangler sat rigid for a long moment, then abruptly clenched his fists.

He stared down at Pembun's tortured face. At that moment he felt himself willing to risk the forcing procedures he had planned to use on Cassina, forgetting the consequences; but there would be no profit in it. In Cassina's case, the material was there; it was only a question of applying enough force on the proper fulcrum to get it out. Here, either the material did not exist, or it was so well

hidden that the most advanced Empire techniques would
never find a hint of it.

But there had to be something: if not espionage, then
treason.

Spangler said, "Pembun, in a war between the Rithians
and the Empire, which side would your favor?"

"The Empire."

Hoarsely: "But as between the Rithian culture and that
of the Empire, which do you prefer?"

"The Rithi."

"Why?"

"Becawse they 'aven' ossified themselves."

"Explain that."

"They 'aven' overspecialized. They're still yuman, in a
sense of the word that's more meaningful than the natural-
history sense. They're alive in a way that you can't say the
Empire is alive. The Empire is like a robot brain with 'alf
the connections soldered shut. It can't adapt, so it's dying;
but it's still big enough to be dangerous."

Spangler flicked a glance of triumph toward the technician. He said, "I will repeat, in the event of war between
the Rithians and the Empire, which side would you favor?"

Pembun said, "The Empire."

Spangler persisted angrily, "How do you justify that
statement, in the face of your admission that you prefer
Rithian culture to Empire culture?"

"My personal preferences aren' important. It would be
bad for the 'ole yuman race if the Empire cracked up too
soon. The Outworlds aren' strong enough. It's too much to
expect them to 'urry up and make themselves self-sufficient
w'en they can lean on the Empire through trade agreements.
The Empire 'as to be kept alive *now*. In another five centuries or so, it won' matter."

Spangler stared a question at the technician, who signaled: "Emotional index one point seven."

One seven: normal for a true statement of a profound
conviction. A falsehood, spoken against the truth-
compulsion of the drug, would have generated at least 3.0.

So it had all slipped out of his hands again. Pembun's
statement was damaging; it would be a black mark on his

dossier: but it was not criminal. There was nothing in it to justify the interrogation: it was hardly more than Pembun had given freely in that report of his.

Spangler made one more attempt. "From the time I met you at the spaceport to the present, have you ever lied to me?"

A pause. "Yes."

"How many times?"

"Once."

Spangler leaned forward eagerly.

"Give me the details!"

"I tol' you the song, *Odum Pawkee Mont a Mutting*, was 'kind of a saga.' That was true in a way, but I said it to fool you. There's an old song with the same name, that dates from the early days on Man'aven, but that's in the old languages. W'at I sang was a modern version. It's not a folk song, or a saga, it's a political song. Old Man Pawkey is the Empire, an' the cup of cawfee is peace. 'E climbs a mounting, and 'e wears 'imself out, and 'e fights a 'undred battles, and 'e lets 'is farm go to forest, just to get a cup of cawfee—instead of growing the bean in 'is own back yard."

A wave of anger towered and broke over Spangler. When it passed, he found himself standing beside the interrogation table, legs spread and shoulders hunched. There was a stinging sensation in the palm of his right hand and the inner surface of the fingers; and there was a dark-red blotch on Pembun's cheek.

The technician was staring at him, but he looked away when Spangler turned.

"Bring him out of it and then let him go," Spangler said, and strode out of the room.

The screen filled one wall of the room, so that the three-dimensional orthocolor image appeared to be physically present beyond a wall of non-reflecting glass.

Spangler sat a little to right of center, with Gordon at his left. To his right was Colonel Leclerc with his aide; at the far left, sitting a little apart from the others, was Pembun.

Spangler had spoken to Pembun as little as possible since

the interrogation; to be in the same room with him was
almost physically distasteful.

On the ancillary screen before Spangler, Keith-Ingram's
broad gray face was mirrored. The circuit was not two-way,
however; Keith-Ingram was receiving the same tight-beam
image that appeared on the big wall screen, and so were
several heads of other departments and at least one High
Assembly member.

The pictured room did not look like a room at all: it
looked almost exactly like the Rithian garden-city Spangler
had seen in the indoctrination film. There were the bluish
light, the broad-leaved green vines and the serpentine blossoms, with the vague feeling of space beyond; and there,
supported by a crotch of the vine, was a Rithian.

The reconstruction was uncannily good, Spangler admitted; if he had not seen the model at close hand, he would
have believed the thing to be alive.

But something was subtly off-key: some quality of the
light, or configuration of the vine stalks, or perhaps even
the attitude of the lifelike Rithian simulacrum. The room as
a whole was like a museum reconstruction: convincing only
after you had voluntarily taken the first step toward belief.

Leclerc was chatting noisily with his aide: his way of
minimizing tension, evidently. The aide nodded and
coughed nervously. Gordon shifted his position, and sub-
sided guiltily when Spangler glanced at him.

Keith-Ingram's lips moved soundlessly; he was talking to
one of the high executives on another circuit. Then the sound
cut in and he said, ''All ready at this end, Spangler. Go
ahead.''

''Right, sir.'' Distastefully, Spangler turned his head toward Pembun. ''Mr. Pembun?''

Pembun spoke quietly into his intercom. A moment later,
the vines at the left side of the room parted and Cassina
stepped into view.

His face was pale and he looked acutely uncomfortable.
Under forced healing techniques he had made a good recovery, but he still looked unwell. He glanced down at the
interlaced vines that concealed the true floor, took two steps

forward, turned to face the motionless Rithian, and assumed the "at ease" position, hands behind his back. His stiff face eloquently expressed disapproval and discomfort.

No one in the viewing room moved or seemed to breathe. Even the restless Leclerc sat statue-still, gazing intently at the screen.

How does Cassina feel, Spangler wondered irrelevantly, with a bomb inside his skull?

Leclerc had set his watch to announce seconds. The tiny ticks were distinctly audible.

Three seconds went by, and nothing happened. Theoretically, if the buried message in Cassina's brain were triggered by the situation, the buried material would come out verbally, with compulsive force.

Four seconds.

Pembun bent forward over his intercom and murmured. In the room of the image the Rithian dummy moved slightly—tentacles gripped and relaxed, shifting its weight minutely; the head turned. A high-pitched voice, apparently coming from the dummy, said, "Enter and be at peace."

Six seconds.

The watch ticked once more; then the dummy spoke again, in the sibilants and harsh fricatives of the Rithian language.

Nine seconds. Ten. The dummy spoke once more in Rithian.

Twelve seconds.

The dummy said in Standard, "You will take some refreshment?"

Cassina's expression did not change; his lips remained shut.

Pembun sighed. "It's no use going on," he said. "I'm afraid it's a failure."

"No luck, Chief," said Spangler. "Pembun says that's all he can do."

Keith-Ingram nodded. "Very well, I'll contact you later. Clearing." His screen went blank.

Pembun was speaking into the intercom. A moment later a voice from behind the vines called, "That's all, Colonel."

Cassina turned and walked stiffly out. "Clearing," said the voice; and the big screen faded to silvery blankness.

Spangler sat still, savoring his one victory, while the others stood up and moved murmuring toward the door. Vines, he thought mockingly. Dummy monsters. Smells!

The next time, it was very different.

Cassina lay clipped and swathed in the interrogation harness. His glittering eyes stared with an expression of frozen terror at the ceiling.

Spangler, at the bedside, was only partly conscious of the other men in the room and of the avid bank of vision cameras. He watched Cassina as one who marks the oily ripples of the ocean's surface, knowing that fathoms under, a gigantic submarine battle is being fought.

In the submerged depths of Cassina's mind, a three-sided struggle had been going on for more than half an hour without a respite. The field of battle centered around a locked and sealed compartment of Cassina's memory. The three combatants were the interrogation machine, the repressive complex which guarded the sealed memory, and Cassina's own desperate will to survive.

The dynamics of the battle were simple and deadly. First, through normal interrogation, Cassina's attention had been directed to the memory-sector in question. The pattern of that avenue of thought was reproduced in the interrogation machine—its jagged outline performed an endless, shuddering dance in the scope—and fed back rhythmically into Cassina's brain, so that his consciousness was redirected, like a compass needle to a magnet, each time it tried to escape. This technique, without the addition of truth drugs or suggestion, was commonly used to recover material suppressed by neurosis or psychic trauma; the interval between surges of current was so calculated that stray bits of the buried memory would be forced out by the repressive mechanism itself—each successive return of attention, therefore, found more of the concealed matter exposed, and complete recall could usually be forced in a matter of seconds.

In Cassina's case, the repressive complex was so strong that these ejected fragments of memory were being reabsorbed almost as fast as they were emitted. The repression was survival-linked, meaning to say that the unreasoning, magical nine-tenths of Cassina's mind was utterly convinced that to give up the buried material was to die. Therefore the battle was being fought two against one: the repressive complex, plus the will to survive, against the interrogation machine.

The machine had two aids: the drugs in Cassina's system, and the tireless, pitiless mechanical voice in his ears: "*Tell!* . . . *Tell!* . . . *Tell!* . . . *Tell!*"

And the power of the machine, unlike that of Cassina's mind, was unlimited.

Cassina's lips worked soundlessly for an instant; then his expression froze again. Spangler waited for another few seconds, and nodded to the technician.

The technician moved his rheostat over another notch.

Seventy times a second, blasting down Cassina's feeble resistance, the feedback current swung his mind back to a single polarity. Cassina could not even escape into insanity, while that circuit was open; there was no room in his mind for any thought but the one, amplified to a mental scream, that tore through his head with each cycle of the current.

The repression complex and the will to survive were constants; the artificial compulsion to remember was a variable.

Spangler nodded again; up went the power.

Cassina's waxen face was shiny with sweat, and so contorted that it was no longer recognizable. Abruptly his eyes closed, and the muscles of his face went slack. The technician darted a glance to one of the dials on his control board, and slammed over a lever. Two signal lights began to flash alternately: Cassina's heart, which had stopped, was being artificially controlled.

An attendant gave Cassina an injection. In a few moments his faced contorted again, and his eyes blinked open.

The silence in the room was absolute. Spangler waited while long minutes ticked away, then nodded to the technician again. The power went up. Again: another notch.

Without warning, Cassina's eyes screwed themselves shut, his jaws distended, and he spoke: a single, formless stream of syllables.

Then his face froze into an icy, indifferent mask. The signal lights continued to flash until the technician, with a tentative gesture, cut the heart-stimulating current; then the steady ticking of the indicator showed that Cassina's heart was continuing to beat on its own. But his face might have been that of a corpse.

Spangler felt his body relax in a release of tension that was almost painful. His fingers trembled. At his nod, the technician cut his master switch and the attendant began removing the harness from Cassina's head and body.

Spangler glanced once at the small vision screen that showed Keith-Ingram's intent face, then took the spool the technician handed him, inserted it into the playback in front of him, and ran it through again and again, first at normal speed, then slowed down so that individual words and syllables could be sorted out.

Cassina had shouted, "You will forget what I am about to tell you and will only remember and repeat the message when you see a Rithian and smell this exact odor. If anyone else tries to make you remember, you will die. *Vuyown fowkip tiima Kreth Grana yodg pirup* pet shop *vuyown geckyg odowo coyowod, cpgnvib btui tene* book store *ikpyu. Nobcyeu kivpi cyour myoc. Aoprosu . . .*"

There was much more of it, all in outlandish syllables except that "pet shop" was repeated once more. The others crowded around, careful only not to obstruct Keith-Ingram's view, while Spangler, pointedly ignoring Pembun, turned the spool over to Heissler, the rabbity little Rithian expert who had been flown in early that morning from Denver.

Heissler listened to the spool once more, made hieroglyphic notes, frowned, and cleared his throat. "This is what it says, *roughly*," he began. "I don't want to commit myself to an exact translation until I've had time to study the text *thoroughly*." He glanced around, then looked down at his notes.

"On the map we sent you by Kreth Grana you will find a pet shop on a north-south avenue, with a restaurant on one side of it and a book store on the other. The first bomb is at this location. The others will be found as follows: from the first location through the outermost projection of the adjacent coastline—'' Heissler paused. "A distance, in Rithian terminology, which is roughly equal to six thousand seven hundred kilometers. I'll work it out exactly in a moment . . . it comes to six seven six eight kilometers, three hundred twenty-nine meters and some odd centimeters—to the second location, which is also a pet shop. From this location, at an interior angle of—let's see, that would be eighty-seven degrees, about eight minutes—yes, eight minutes, six seconds—here's another distance, which works out to . . . ah, nine thousand three hundred seventy-two kilometers, one meter—to the third location. From this location, at an exterior angle of ninety-three degrees, twenty minutes, two seconds . . ."

Spangler palmed his intercom, got Miss Timoney, and directed her: "Get street maps of all major North American cities and put all the available staff to work on them, starting with those over five million. They are to look for a pet shop—that's right, a *pet shop*—on a north-south avenue, which has a restaurant on one side of it and a book store on the other. This project is to be set up as temporary but has triple-A priority. In the meantime, rough out a replacement project to cover all inhabited areas in this hemisphere, staff to be adequate to finish the task in not over forty-eight hours—and have the outline on my desk for approval when I come back to the office."

". . . seven thousand nine hundred eighty-one kilometers, ninety-eight meters, to the fifth location. Message ends." Heissler folded his hands and sat back.

Spangler glanced at Keith-Ingram. The gray man nodded. "Good work, Thorne! Keep that project of yours moving and I'll see to it that similar ones are set up in the other districts. Congratulations to you all. Clearing." His screen faded.

. . . And that was it, Spangler thought. Undoubtedly there were millions of pet shops in the world which had a restaurant on one side and a book store on the other, and were on north-south avenues; but there couldn't be many pairs of them on a line whose exact distance was known, and which passed through the salient point of a coastline adjacent to the first. It was just the sort of mammoth problem with

which the Empire was superlatively equipped to deal. Within
two days, the bombs would have been found and deacti-
vated.

Curiously, it was not his inevitable promotion which
occupied Spangler's mind at that moment, not even the certainty that the Empire's most terrible danger had been
averted. He was thinking about Pembun.

In more ways than one, he thought, this is the victory of
reason over sentiment, science over witchcraft. *This is the
historic triumph of the single meaning.*

He glanced at Pembun, still sitting by himself at the end
of the room. The little man's face was gray under the brown.
He was hunched over, staring at nothing.

Spangler watched him, feeling the void inside himself
where triumph should have been. It was always like this,
after he had won. So long as the fight lasted, Spangler was
a vessel of hatred; when it was all over, when his emotions
had done their work, they flowed out of him and left him at
peace. Sometimes it was difficult to remember how he
could have thought the defeated enemy so important, how
he could have burned with impotent rage at the very existence of a man so small, so shriveled, so obviously harm-
less. Sometimes, as now, Spangler felt the intrusive touch
of compassion.

It's how we're made, he thought. The next objective is
always the important thing, the only thing that exists for us
. . . and then, when we've reached it, we wonder why it
was so necessary, and sometimes we don't know quite what
to do with it. But there's always something else to fight for.
It may be childish, but it's the thing that makes us great.

Pembun stood up slowly and walked over to Colonel Leclerc, who was talking ebulliently to Gordon. Spangler saw
Leclerc turn and listen to something Pembun was saying;
then his eyebrows arched roguishly and he shook his head,
putting a finger to his pursed lips. Pembun spoke again, and
Leclerc grinned hugely, leaned over and whispered something into Pembun's ear, then shouted with laughter.

Pembun walked out of the room, glancing at Spangler as
he passed. His face was still gray, but there was a faint,
twisted smile on his lips.

He's made a joke, Spangler thought. Give him credit for courage.

He felt suddenly listless, as he had been after the scene with Joanna. He moved toward the door, but a sudden tingling of uneasiness made him hesitate. He turned after a moment and walked over to Leclerc.

"Pardon my curiosity, Colonel," he said. "What was it that Pembun said to you just now?"

Leclerc's eyes glistened. "He was very droll. He asked me if I knew any French, and I said yes—I spoke it as a child, you know; I grew up in a very backward area. Well, then he asked me if it was not true that in French 'pet shop' would have an entirely different meaning than in Standard." He snickered.

"And you told him—?" Spangler prompted.

Leclerc made one of his extravagant gestures. "I said yes! That is, if you take the first word to be French, and the second to be Standard, then a pet shop would be—" he lowered his voice to a dramatic undertone—"a shop that sold impolite noises."

He laughed immoderately, shaking his head. "What a thing to think of!"

Spangler smiled wryly. "Thank you, Colonel," he said, and walked out. That touch of uneasiness had been merely a hangover, he thought; it was no longer necessary to worry about anything that Pembun said, or thought, or did.

Pembun was waiting for him in his outer office.

Spangler looked at him without surprise, and crossed the room to sit beside him. "Yes, Mr. Pembun?" he said simply.

"I 'ave something to tell you," Pembun said, "that you won't like to 'ear. Per'aps we'd better go inside."

"All right," said Spangler, and led the way.

He found himself walking along a deserted corridor on the recreation level. On one side, the doorways he passed beckoned him with stereos of the tri-D's to be experienced inside—a polar expedition on Nereus VI, an evening with Ayesha O'Shaughnessy, a nightmare, a pantomime, a ballet, a battle in space. On the other, he glimpsed the pale, crystalline shells of empty dream capsules.

He did not know how long he had been walking. He had boarded a scooter, he remembered, but he did not know which direction he had taken, or how long he had ridden, or where he had got off. His feet ached, so he must have been walking quite a long time.

He glanced upward. The ceiling of the corridor was stereocelled, and the view that was turned on now was that of the night sky: a clear, cold night, by the look of it; a sky of deep jet, each star as brilliant and sharp as a kernel of ice.

Pembun's gray-brown face stared back at him from the sky. He had been watching that face ever since he had left his office; he had seen it against the satin-polished walls of corridors; it was there when he closed his eyes; but it looked singularly appropriate against this background. The stars have Pembun's face, he thought.

A bone-deep shudder went through his body. He turned aside and went into one of the dream rooms, and sat down on the robing bench. The door closed obsequiously behind him.

He looked down into the open capsule, softly padded and just big enough for a man to lie snugly; he touched its midnight-blue lining. The crystal curve of the top was like ice carved paper-thin; the gas vents were lipped by circlets of rose-finished metal, antiseptically bright.

No, he thought. At least, not yet. I've got to think.

A pun, a pun, a beastly, moronic pun . . .

Pembun had said, "I've made a bad mistake, Commissioner. You remember me asking w'y Colonel Cassina tried so 'ard to get to the Rithch w'en 'e saw we'd found 'im out?"

And Spangler, puzzled, uneasy: "I remember."

"An' I answered myself, that Cassina must 'ave been ordered to do it so that 'e could be killed—becawse of the message in 'is brain that the Rithch wouldn' want us to find."

"You were right, Mr. Pembun."

"No, I was wrong. I ought to 'ave seen it. We know that

the Ritch's post-'ypnotic control over Cassina was strong enough to make 'im try to commit suicide; 'e almost succeeded later on, even though we 'ad 'im under close observation and were ready for it. So it wouldn't 'ave made sense for the Ritch to order 'im to come and be killed. If Cassina 'ad tried to kill *imself*, right then, the minute we came into the office, there isn' any doubt that 'e would 'ave been able to do it. We never could 'ave stopped 'im in time.''

Spangler's brain had clung to that unanswerable syllogism, and gone around and around with it, and come out nowhere. ''What are you getting at?''

''Don't you see, Commissioner? W'at the Ritch rilly wanted was w'at actually 'appened. 'E wanted us to kill *'im*—because it was in 'is brain, not in Cassina's, that the rilly dangerous information was.''

Pembun had paused. Then: ''They love life. 'E couldn' bring 'imself to do it, but 'e could arrange it so that we'd be sure to kill 'im, not take 'im alive.''

And Spangler, hoarsely: ''Are you saying that that message we got from Cassina was a fraud?''

''No. It might be, but I don' think so. I think the Ritch left the genuine message in Cassina's mind, all right, for a joke—and becawse 'e knew that even if we found it, it wouldn' do us any good.''

Spangler had hardly recognized his own voice. ''I don't understand you. What are you trying to—What do you mean, it wouldn't do us any good?''

No triumph in Pembun's voice, only weariness and regret: ''I told you you wouldn' like it, Commissioner. Did you notice there were two Standard phrases in that message?''

''Pet shop and book store. Well?''

''You can say the same things in Rochtik—*brutu ka* and *lessi ka*. They're exact translations; there wouldn' 'ave been any danger of confusion at awl.''

Spangler had stared at him, silently, for a long moment. Inside him, he had felt as if the solid earth had fallen away beneath him, all but a slender pinnacle on which he sat perched; as if he had to be very careful not to make any sudden motion, lest he slip and tumble down the precipice.

"Did you know," he asked, "that I would ask Colonel Leclerc what you said to him?"

Pembun nodded: "I thought you might. I thought per'aps it would prepare you, a little. This isn' easy to take."

"What are you waiting for?" Spangler had managed. "Tell me the rest."

"*Pet* 'appens to be a sound that's used in a good many languages. In Late Terran French it 'as an impolite meaning. But in Twalaz, w'ich is derived from French, it means 'treasure,' and a pet shop would be w'at you cawl a jewelry store.

"Then there's Kah-rin, w'ich is the trade language in the Goren system and some others. In Kah-rin, *pet* means a toupee. And as for 'book store,' *book* means 'machine' in Yessuese, 'carpet' in Elda, 'toy' in Baluat—and *bukstor* means 'public urinal' in Perroschi. Those are just a few that I 'appen to know; there are prob'ly a 'undred others that I never 'eard of.

"Prob'ly the Rithi agreed on w'at language or dialect to use before they came 'ere. It's the kind of thing that would amuse them. . . . I'm sorry. I told you they liked puns, Commissioner . . . and you know that Earth is the only yuman planet w'ere the language 'asn't evolved in the last four 'undred years. . . .''

Now he understood why Pembun's face was gray: not because Spangler had defeated him in a contest of wills—but because the Empire had had its deathblow.

Night upon night, deep after endless deep; distance without perspective, relation without order: the Universe without the Empire.

One candle, that they had thought would burn forever, now snuffed out and smoking in the darkness.

Another deep shudder racked Spangler's body. Blindly, he crawled into the capsule and closed it over him.

After a long time, he opened his eyes and saw two blurred faces looking in at him. The light hurt his eyes. He blinked until he could see them clearly: one was Pembun and the other was Joanna.

" 'Ow long 'as 'e been in there?" Pembun's voice said.

"I don't know, there must be something wrong with the machine. The dials aren't registering at all." Joanna's voice, but sounding as he had never heard it before. "If the shutoff didn't work—"

"Better cawl a doctor."

"Yes." Joanna's head turned aside and vanished.

"Wait," Spangler said thickly. He struggled to sit up.

Joanna's head reappeared, and both of them stared at him, as if he were a specimen that had unexpectedly come to life. It made Spangler want to laugh.

"Security," he said. "Security has been shot out from under me. That is a pun."

Joanna choked and turned away. After a moment Spangler realized that she was crying. He shook his head violently to clear it and started to climb out of the capsule. Pembun put a hand on his arm.

"Can you 'ear me, Thorne?" he said anxiously. "Do you understand w'at I'm saying?"

"I'm all right," said Spangler, standing up. "Joanna, what's the matter with you?"

She turned. "You're not—"

"I'm all right. I was tired, and I crawled in there to rest. I stayed there, thinking, for an hour or so. Then I must have fallen asleep."

She took one step and was pressed tight against him, her cheek against his throat, her arms clutching him fiercely. Her body trembled.

"You were gone six hours," Pembun said "I got Miss Planter's name from your emergency listing, and we've been looking for you ever since. I shouldn' 'ave jumped to conclusions, I guess." He turned to go.

"Wait," said Spangler again. He felt weak, but very clear-headed and confident. "Please. I have something to say to you."

Joanna pulled away from him abruptly and began hunting for a tissue. Spangler got one out of his pouch and handed it to her.

"Thanks," she said in a small voice, and sat down on the bench.

"This is for you, too, Joanna," said Spangler soberly. "Part of it." He turned to Pembun.

"You were wrong," he said.

Pembun's face slowly took on a resigned expression. "'Ow?"

"You told me, under interrogation, that your only reason for working with the Empire, against its rivals, was that the Empire was necessary to the Outworlds—that if it broke up too soon, the Outworlds would not be strong enough to stand by themselves."

"If you say so, I'll take your word for it, Commissioner."

"You said it. Do you deny it now?"

"No."

"You were wrong. You justified your position by saying that the Outworlds would be forced to overspecialize, like the Empire, in order to break away from it . . . that the cure would be worse than the disease. You've given your life to work that must have been distasteful to you, every minute of it." He took a deep breath. "I can't imagine why, unless you were reasoning on the basis of two assumptions that a twenty-first century schoolboy could have disproved—that like causes invariably produce like results, and that the end justifies the means."

Pembun's expression changed from boredom to surprise, to shock, to incredulous surmise. Now he looked at Spangler as if he had never seen him before. "Go awn," he said softly.

"Instead of staying on Manhaven, where you belonged, you've been bumbling about the Empire, trying to hold together a structure that needed only one push in the right place to bring it down. . . . You've been as wrong as I was. Both of us have been wasting our lives.

"Now see what's happened! Earth is finished as a major power. The Empire is dead this minute, though it may not begin to stink for another century. The Outworlds have *got* to stand alone. If like measures produce like ends, then that's the way it will be, whether you like it or not—but history never repeats itself, Pembun."

"Jawj," said the little man.

"—Jawj. Incidentally, I know you dislike apologies—"

"You don't owe me any," said Pembun. They smiled at each other with the embarrassment of men who have discovered a liking for each other. Then Spangler thrust out his hand and Pembun took it.

"Thorne, what are you going to do?" Joanna asked.

He looked at her. "Resign tomorrow, get a visa as soon as I can, and ship out. If I can find a place that will take me."

"There's a place for you on Man'aven," said Pembun. "If there isn't, we'll make one."

Joanna looked from one to the other, and said nothing.

"Jawj," said Spangler, "wait for us outside a few minutes, will you?"

The little man grinned happily, sketched a bow, and walked out. His voice floated back: "I'll be with Miss O'Shaughnessy w'en you wawnt me."

Spangler sat down beside Joanna. She looked at him with an expression in which bewilderment and pain were mingled with something else, harder to define.

"Miss O'Shaughnessy?" she asked.

"One of the tri-D's across the corridor. I wonder if he has any idea of what he's getting into." He paused. "I have something else to say to you, Joanna."

"Thorne, if it's an apology—"

"It isn't. If Pembun told you anything about the last few days, then perhaps you understand part of the reason for— what I did."

"Yes."

"But that's nothing. What I have to tell you is that I made up my mind to marry you three months ago . . . not because you're Joanna . . . but because you're a Planter."

"I knew that."

Spangler stared at her. "You what?"

"Why else do you think I wouldn't?' she demanded, meeting his gaze.

Her cheeks were flushed, her eyes glittering with the remnants of tears. The aloof, icy mask was gone. She looked, Spangler discovered, nothing whatever like a statue of Aristocracy.

"Will you come with me?"

She looked down. "Will you go without me, if I don't?"

". . . Yes," said Spangler. "I've got a lot to do, and a lot to make up for. Thirty years. I can't do it here."

"In that case," Joanna said, "—you'll have to persuade me, won't you?"